devious

it girl novels created by Cecily von Ziegesar:

The It Girl
Notorious
Reckless
Unforgettable
Lucky
Tempted
Infamous
Adored
Devious

If you like **the it girl**, you may also enjoy:

The **Poseur** series by Rachel Maude
The **Secrets of My Hollywood Life** series by Jen Calonita
Betwixt by Tara Bray Smith
Haters by Alisa Valdes-Rodriguez
Footfree and Fancyloose by Elizabeth Craft and Sarah Fain

devious

an it girl novel

CREATED BY
CECILY VON ZIEGESAR

poppy

LITTLE, BROWN AND COMPANY
New York   Boston

Poppy

Hachette Book Group
237 Park Avenue, New York, NY 10017
For more of your favorite series, go to www.pickapoppy.com

First Edition: November 2009

Poppy is an imprint of Little, Brown Books for Young Readers.
The Poppy name and logo are trademarks of Hachette Book Group, Inc.

alloyentertainment
Produced by Alloy Entertainment
151 West 26th Street, New York, NY 10001

Cover design by Andrea C. Uva
Cover photograph by Roger Moenks

ISBN: 978-0-316-07394-3
10 9 8 7 6 5 4 3 2 1
CWO
Printed in the United States of America

If you obey all the rules, you miss all the fun.

—Katharine Hepburn

A WAVERLY OWL ALWAYS WELCOMES NEW
STUDENTS TO THE WAVERLY COMMUNITY.

The chapel bell tolled on that cold January morning, alerting the Waverly Academy student body that there were only five minutes before the dean's first address of the brand-new year. Jenny Humphrey took a deep breath of crisp air as she bolted down one of the salted paths crisscrossing the snow-covered quad. Her fleece-lined Camper boots crunched against the snow, and the ends of the long gold-and-white scarf her mother had sent from Prague trailed behind her like a flag. It was the Monday morning after Christmas break, and the scene was still unblemished by footprints and snowball fights. The sloping roofs of the brick school buildings were covered in white, looking like so many gingerbread houses. It made Jenny fall in love with Waverly Academy all over again.

Up ahead, a crowd of students streamed into the stone chapel, eager to get Dean Marymount's welcome-back-to-campus address over with. "You're so tan, Jenny!" Sage Francis exclaimed, waving from the top of the stairs. Her pin-straight corn silk–blond hair stuck out from underneath a hand-knit pink-and-white-striped beret. "I can't believe you got to spend two weeks in the Bahamas with the Vernons."

"Your freckles really came out." Benny Cunningham eyed Jenny critically as she expertly tied her striped Waverly tie into a perfect Windsor knot. It had taken Jenny about twenty tries in front of the mirror to get her own knot right. Benny's camel Michael Kors coat flapped open over her regulation maroon Waverly blazer. Marymount's first chapel address meant everyone had to dress alike—at least for the morning.

"Just one week," Jenny corrected Sage, ignoring Benny's passive-aggressive freckle comment as the girls waited for the crowd to move through the door. She'd spent Christmas in New York with her dad, Rufus, and brother, Dan, and then a week with Callie Vernon, her beautiful Southern belle roommate, at her family's retreat in Nassau. As they packed to go home for break, Callie had begged her to come along on their family vacation, not wanting to be left alone with her parents. Jenny was a little intimidated by the idea of spending a week with Callie's glamorous Georgia-governor mother and international real estate magnate father. But they'd been surprisingly easygoing, spending the days on their laptops and cell phones and letting the girls do as they pleased—which mostly consisted of parking their rattan beach mats on the warm sand and soaking up the sun. Jenny made her way through the condo's complete collection of Agatha Christie books as well as two whole tubes of Neutrogena Ultra Sheer sunblock.

"Really, I hope you used lotion with a high SPF," Benny, whose pale skin looked downright Casperesque, added. The three girls elbowed their way through the heavy oak doorway into the chapel. "Tropical sun practically guarantees skin cancer and wrinkles," she said with a tone of authority.

Jenny almost laughed. At Constance Billard, her old school back in New York City, she was always jealous of her classmates who came back tanned and gorgeous from their breaks in Palm Beach or St. Lucia. Now, she was actually one of them.

"Grab your seats, Owls!" Ms. Rose, Jenny's English teacher, directed. She clapped her hands and attempted to shepherd the slow-moving students inside. Even the faculty was required to wear their regulation blazers and ties for the first chapel meeting, and the petite teacher could easily have passed for a student.

The high-ceilinged chapel was warm and humid. The aisles were crowded with boys in wrinkled blazers, slapping one another's backs and exchanging elaborate knuckle-bumping handshakes. Girls hugged and chattered about their family trips to Anguilla or Aspen.

"Jenny!" Alison Quentin, Jenny's friend from art class, called to her from a bench near the front of the chapel. "I saved you a seat."

Jenny squeezed past a pack of giggling soccer team girls admiring the diamond-encrusted tennis bracelet on Rifat Jones's wrist. She slid onto the hard wooden bench next to Alison. "How was your break?" Jenny asked, unwinding her scarf from her neck. She shook some melting snow off her long brown curls. "You were in Connecticut, right?"

"Boring. So glad to be back to civilization." Alison rolled her eyes and pushed up the frayed sleeves of her blazer. "Listen, what are you doing for Jan Plan? Verena and I decided last night to write and perform a one-act play, but we need another person to make it work. Do you want in?"

Jan Plan was one of Waverly Academy's greatest institutions. Instead of regular classes, students spent the month of January on campus working on one less-conventional learning project. Most people worked in pairs or small groups, on anything from tracking precipitation patterns in Rhinecliff to writing a paper about the representation of beauty in *Ugly Betty*. There was a handful of classes taught by Waverly profs for the students who couldn't function without the regular class structure, but they were far more fun than your average chem or algebra class: popular choices were Knitting 101, Music Appreciation, and various language immersion courses that meant spending hours in the screening room watching foreign films and eating popcorn. Best of all, students were graded on a pass/fail basis. Which naturally meant sleeping late, and parties every night.

"Thanks for asking," Jenny said, stuffing her pink Gap gloves into her blazer pockets. She shifted her knees to the side to let a bulky football player squeeze past. "But I was kind of hoping to work on this art project I've been thinking about."

After taking two amazing fall-semester art classes—advanced figure drawing and portraiture—Jenny was dying to put what she learned toward a solo art project. Over break, she'd been standing at the corner of Columbus Avenue and Eighty-fifth Street, watching the people stream across the street as the WALK sign blinked on. Wet snow drifted down from the sky, and something about the way the people were moving made Jenny wish she had a camera—or that she *were* a camera. She tried to imagine what the photograph would look like if she left the shutter open: the garbage cans and mailboxes on the sidewalk would stay the same, but the people would be just a beautiful blur of motion. Immediately, she knew she wanted to try and replicate that impression with her own eyes and hands.

Which was going to be tricky, since students were encouraged to work together for Jan Plan. Technically, only juniors and seniors were allowed to work alone with permission from their advisers. "Ms. Rose said I'll need to get permission from Marymount to do it on my own."

Alison ran a tube of cherry ChapStick across her lips. "Good luck. You know what a grouch he can be."

Jenny nodded slowly. She was dreading asking Dean Marymount for permission to work alone on her project, especially since she'd already been in trouble so many times this year. What could she possibly say to make him believe she was a responsible, rule-abiding Owl? "Wait, where is Dean Marymount?" Jenny asked, craning her neck to see if she could spot him up by the stage. The chapel bell had finished chiming five minutes ago, and a murmur ran through the crowd as students began to realize that something wasn't quite right.

"*That* is not Marymount," Alison whispered. The entire student body watched as a tall man with a head of thick steel-gray hair strode confidently across the stage. He was in his late forties, dapper, and looked like he could have played James Bond in a different life—a far cry from the balding, sweater-vest-wearing Dean Marymount. "Is that Armani?" Alison asked, nodding at his expensive-looking suit.

By the time James Bond had reached the podium at the center of the stage, the entire chapel was abuzz with conversation. "Everyone, please." He raised a single hand into the air. "There's no need to panic." The man had a deep, soothing voice, and, as if by magic, the room grew silent. "Dean Marymount is alive and well, but there's been a change in the administration. My name is Dr. Henry Dresden, and I'm your new dean."

The chapel gave a collective gasp.

"Things are going to be a little different with me in charge," Dr. Dresden chuckled, and smoothed his royal blue tie. "I'll be down in the trenches with you. I'll be teaching a class spring semester—Advanced Comp Lit, for those of you unlucky enough to be in it." He gave a half grin to the stunned students.

"Ohmigod. Is it too late to register?" Alison whispered, nudging Jenny sharply in the ribs.

"Also, working among you will be my own children, Isaac and Isla." He tilted his face slightly to smile at a boy and a girl sitting at the edge of the stage. Jenny hadn't noticed them before. They were both about sixteen or seventeen, with dark wavy hair and pale green eyes . . . and incredibly good-looking. They wore maroon Waverly blazers that still had a starched, brand-new look to them.

"Someone answered my prayers." Ryan Reynolds leaned forward against the back of Jenny's pew to punch Lon Baruzza on the arm. "I got dibs on the chick."

Alison rolled her eyes. "Good luck with that." The dean's daughter, whose wavy brown hair looked perfectly tousled, tucked her plaid Burberry skirt tighter around her knees, as if she knew all the boys in the crowd were staring at her.

Jenny turned her eyes to the boy. He was adorable, with dark, slightly curled hair and smooth, tanned skin. Her stomach dropped when she realized he was staring straight at her. A faint smile appeared on his lips, as if he liked what he saw.

Her heart pounded at twice its normal speed. Was she imagining it? The boy's striking green eyes held a playful look, a challenge to hold his gaze. Suddenly, the art project that had seemed so important five minutes ago was the furthest thing from her mind.

Jenny was used to being the new kid on campus, but now she was happy to relinquish the title.

OwlNet

TinsleyCarmichael:	Think Marymount got fired? Or that his wife caught him with Pardee and made him leave Waverly?
CallieVernon:	Who cares? This dean seems so chill.
TinsleyCarmichael:	Too bad he wasn't dean when Easy was around.
CallieVernon:	I know. Maybe then I'd still have a boyfriend.
TinsleyCarmichael:	And his hottie kids? That's not going to hurt his popularity.
CallieVernon:	U have a boyfriend, don't forget. Leave the hotties for us spinsters.

OwlNet

RyanReynolds: I officially call dibs on the dean's daughter.

AlanStGirard: No dice, bro. We all saw her at the same time.

RyanReynolds: That's why I'm calling dibs!

AlanStGirard: Sorry. All's fair in love and hot chicks.

A WAVERLY OWL SEEKS TO UNDERSTAND THE
MYSTERIES OF HUMAN NATURE—ESPECIALLY IF SHE
CAN GET SCHOOL CREDIT FOR IT.

Callie Vernon yawned as she stepped through the oversize
doors of the dining hall. It resembled an old English
cathedral, with thick stone walls and an arched ceiling.
The walls were lined with black-and-white class pictures dating back to Waverly's founding and shots of the campus when
it was little more than two brick buildings and the chapel.
Callie's parents had met at Waverly and were both in one of
the class photographs. It made her both slightly nervous and
slightly annoyed that she couldn't escape their watchful eyes
even a thousand miles away.

Callie dragged her feet over to the cereal bar. She'd found it
almost impossible to get out of bed that morning, her body still
on the sleep-till-noon schedule of her Caribbean vacation. After

pouring herself a bowl of MultiGrain Cheerios and a glass of orange juice, her hazel eyes scanned the breakfast crowd. The hall was a sea of alarmingly similar maroon-clad bodies, and it took her a moment to single out the adorably sun-freckled Jenny, her Bahamian companion, and her other best friend, Tinsley Carmichael. They were sitting at a long oak table in front of the fireplace with Benny and Sage and a bunch of other Dumbarton girls.

"Nice hair," Tinsley said cheerfully, reaching out to flick Callie's messy ponytail. She wore a thin black T-shirt and a pair of narrow-wale black Earl cords. How did Tinsley always manage to just throw things on and still look so good? "Looks like you're still on vacation time."

Callie slid her tray onto the table, her skim milk spilling over the edge of her cereal bowl. "Leave me alone. I'm in sunlight withdrawal."

A dreamy look came across Jenny's wide brown eyes. "I still keep thinking about the warm powdery sand."

"We *get* it already." Benny Cunningham leaned her elbows on the table, twirling her platinum Tiffany rings around her finger. "You guys lounged in the Caribbean while I was stuck in the snow. Can we talk about something else, please?"

Callie eased off her Waverly blazer and set it on the back of her chair. She'd had it since freshman year, and the elbows were wearing thin. "Don't hate me because I'm tan."

Sage Francis giggled as she spread low-fat cream cheese across her toasted onion bagel. "Benny's just bitter that her fam called off their annual trip to Aruba. She had to make do with a week in London instead."

Benny smirked at Sage. "Can you blame me? My skin looks paler than Nicole Kidman's, and now there's this hottie dean's son to impress." She tossed her banana peel onto Sage's tray. "We should invite him to work on our Jan Plan project with us."

Sage stuffed the banana peel into Benny's half-empty water glass. "What's his name? Ivan?"

Callie exchanged a raised eyebrow with Tinsley, who was languidly mixing strawberries into her plain yogurt. Benny and Sage had a history of throwing themselves at any new guy who stepped on campus. Usually they wound up scaring him off.

"Isaac, I think." Jenny spoke up, glancing around the crowded dining hall as if to check for his presence.

Callie eyed her petite, curvy roommate. It had been fun to have Jenny with her on vacation. Tinsley had had other plans for break—involving her glued-to-the-hip boyfriend, Julian— and the thought of hanging out alone with her parents made Callie hyperventilate. Jenny was laid back and easy to please. And even though she drew a fair amount of stares on the beach in her cute navy polka-dotted J. Crew suit, slender Callie, in her sexy black-and-gold Dior string bikini, didn't feel threatened. She owned that beach—at least for a week.

"Hey, what are you guys doing for your Jan Plan projects?" Callie changed the subject. Jan Plan was everyone's favorite time of year. It was four weeks of heaven: you got to be on campus with your friends and not have any real responsibilities. Some of the students were away—like Brett Messerschmidt, another one of Callie's best friends, who was in New York working on a *Vogue* internship her sister had arranged. The nerdier students tended to have more academic plans, like performing a mock trial or spending the whole month reading a horribly long, boring classic novel from the seventeenth century and writing a paper about how it was still relevant today. Callie didn't get why anyone would work so hard for a pass/fail grade. "I still don't have one yet."

Sage twirled a piece of her pale blond hair around her finger. "Benny and I are going to be studying gender roles in contemporary film."

Tinsley, who acted scandalized anytime someone suggested watching a movie that wasn't either black-and-white or filmed in another language, took a small sip of grapefruit juice and rolled her eyes. "So you're using it as an excuse to watch *Made of Honor* for the billionth time?"

"Among other things," Benny trilled. She waved over Emily Jenkins, who was stuffing pieces of fruit into her pockets. "Emily's going to be studying the effects of exercise on stress."

"Groundbreaking," Tinsley whispered to Callie, who almost choked on her orange juice.

"I'm leading a Pilates class on Mondays, Wednesdays, and Fridays in the dance studio, in case anyone's interested," Emily offered, wrapping her scarf tighter around her neck. "I can't believe this counts as school."

"Neither can I," Callie replied dryly, slicing up a banana into her bowl of Cheerios. Of course Emily Jenkins would use Jan Plan as a way to drop a jeans size.

"You ready to go back?" Benny stood up, throwing her

crumpled napkin onto her tray. "I thought maybe we'd watch *27 Dresses* to warm us up."

Tinsley made a gagging sound in her throat as the three girls disappeared. "At least Brett's doing something cool. I can't believe she's got an internship at *Vogue*."

"Yeah, but it's weird she'll be away." Jenny wiped a smudge of raspberry jam off her cheek. "I bumped into Sebastian in Maxwell last night and he looked miserable."

Now *Callie* wanted to throw up. "I can't *believe* how off track I was with that whole Sebastian thing." It was hard to believe that just a month ago, she was—kind of—dating Sebastian Valenti herself. That "relationship" was a perfect example of Callie convincing herself of something that didn't really exist. She'd believed in unicorns until she was eleven, despite all evidence to the contrary, simply because she'd wanted to. Bored and lonely after breaking up with Easy Walsh, she'd suddenly felt like she was destined to be alone. She'd needed a boyfriend.

And then Sebastian had strolled into the room, representing a world of opportunity. A blank slate. Of course, Callie didn't realize he was Brett's tutee the first time she saw him—or that Brett had already set her sights on him. Callie had thrown herself at Sebastian, ignoring his less-appealing qualities, only to end up getting dumped for Brett, with whom he'd been in love the whole time. "The funny thing is—I didn't even really like him. I mean, his idea of romantic was Bon Jovi and pizza. Ew." Callie shook her head as if to shake off the memory.

"You certainly did a good job convincing yourself of it," Tinsley pointed out. Tinsley latched and unlatched the antique platinum chain bracelet she wore around her wrist—probably a romantic Christmas present from her boyfriend, Julian McCafferty. Callie consoled herself with the fact that Julian was a freshman. He didn't even have a learner's permit yet.

"That's what's so weird about it." Callie shifted in her seat as she flicked an imaginary piece of lint off her blazer. "I didn't *feel* like I was convincing myself. He was hot, and everybody was drooling over him. Plus, I was starting to feel frantic about being alone. And then everything just kind of came together. . . ."

"You can't really think you'll be alone forever." Jenny's brown doe eyes widened. She looked tiny in her pink striped button-down and her Waverly blazer, the sleeves of which were a little too long for her.

"I don't know. It's just that I thought Easy was my true love, and then . . . it ended," Callie replied. She stared at the Cheerios floating in her skim milk. She'd always thought she and Easy would be together forever. But after he was expelled from Waverly, he practically disappeared from her life. His father had condemned him to a military school in the middle of the boonies, where he didn't have access to e-mail or a phone. It was too difficult to keep a relationship going when she couldn't ever see him—or even *talk* to him. By the time he sneaked away from school to meet her on Thanksgiving atop the Empire State Building, it was too late. Callie didn't totally understand why, but she knew it was over. "Does that mean it wasn't really true love? Or did I convince myself about Easy the same way I tricked myself into liking Sebastian?"

"Sounds like a brilliant psychology project to me." Tinsley spread some Foul Play NARS gloss across her lips.

"I could totally do a Jan Plan project about the nature of love." Callie straightened in her chair. "Is it something we cling to, just because it offers comfort? Do we have the power to convince ourselves we're in love? Or is it a stronger feeling, one we can't control?" Suddenly a wave of excitement washed over her. She flashed forward twenty years, to herself as a brilliant, Ivy League–educated love expert and best-selling author, signing books to adoring fans, many of whom happened to be male and gorgeous.

"I was being sarcastic," Tinsley pointed out, taking a sip of her tea.

"I wasn't." Callie shrugged. "I want to talk to other people. Find out what makes them think they're in love with someone." Her eyes narrowed and focused on Tinsley, as she gathered up her bag and tossed her crumpled napkin on her tray. "You can be my first victim."

Tinsley smiled sweetly and stood up. "Sorry, babe." She tossed her head, her silky dark hair shimmering under the dining-hall lights. "You know I don't like to kiss and tell."

Callie snorted. "You *love* to kiss and tell."

Tinsley's blue-violet eyes twinkled. "Yeah, I guess I do. Speaking of kissing, I've got to go make out with Julian right now." She blew Callie a kiss as she headed for the dining hall's front doors.

Callie sniffed. True love was definitely something people made up just to annoy her.

A WAVERLY OWL ACTIVELY PURSUES CHARACTER-BUILDING EXPERIENCES.

Brett Messerschmidt stared out the vast plate glass windows of the *Vogue* waiting room on the twelfth floor of the Condé Nast Building in Times Square. Having a sister who worked in the fashion magazine industry definitely had it perks: everything from free samples to seats at runway shows. Now, sitting on an uncomfortable ultramodern leather chair and gazing out at the endless traffic of a Monday morning in January, it was really sinking in. Brett's older sister, Brianna, was an editorial assistant at *Elle*, and last week, over cocktails, her Vassar friend Leslie Nichols, an editorial assistant at *Vogue*, had been complaining about her workload. Her latest intern had disappeared while out getting coffee, taking the petty cash with her. Brianna had immediately suggested Brett for the job. It was perfect for Brett—fashion fascinated her, and she'd always dreamed of becoming a globe-trotting journalist. What

better start than an internship at *Vogue*? Besides, Waverly loved
when its students used Jan Plan to score high-profile, résumé-
boosting internships. After a quick phone interview with a
frazzled Leslie, Brett was hired for the month of January.

It had all happened so quickly, Brett barely had time to
think about it. Which was fortunate, since she probably would
have started feeling sorry for herself. Of course the chance to
spend a glamorous month in New York would come up only
after she began an incredible new relationship with Sebastian
Valenti, who'd be at Waverly this month, *without* her.

Christmas break had been amazing. For once, her parents'
New Jersey accents and need to have at least two televisions on
in the house at all times didn't even faze her. She spent most of
her time with Sebastian, the handsome dark-haired, dark-eyed
senior whom she'd spent the past two months tutoring—and
falling for. Her parents' house in Rumson was about twenty
minutes away from his, and they'd gone back and forth between
each other's houses daily. She'd played a string of backgammon
games with his father, who talked like he was on *The Sopranos*
but was as gentle as a kitten. Sebastian had watched corny movies on the Messerschmidts' beloved fifty-eight-inch plasma TV.
They'd even taken a trip to the Jersey shore and walked along
the cold, quiet beaches, holding hands and peering into the
shops, arcades, and tattoo parlors that were shuttered for the
season.

"Brett?"

She immediately jumped to her feet, smoothing down the
poppy-colored Nanette Lepore bubble skirt she'd borrowed

from Bree. She'd paired it with her favorite cream-colored ruffle-front blouse, then added a cropped navy Diesel jacket with oversize gold buttons and a pair of her sister's brown leather ankle boots. Bree had insisted on rewatching *The Devil Wears Prada* the night before for good luck. Brett couldn't help feeling a little like Anne Hathaway—*after* her transformation into a fashion maven, of course.

"I'm Leslie." In front of her was a tall blonde with a sharp, birdlike face. "So nice to finally meet you."

Brett smiled as she shook Leslie's manicured hand, a giant emerald green bangle clattering on Leslie's wrist. "It's really great to be here. Thank you so much for this opportunity."

A strange look crossed Leslie's pretty face before she smiled brightly again. "Can I get you some coffee or anything? Tea? Water?" Leslie spoke in a clipped, rapid-fire way, as if she was already thinking about the millions of things she had to do that morning.

"I'm fine, thank you," Brett demurred, suspecting that Leslie was just being polite. She grabbed her cream-colored Chanel quilted purse and slid it over her shoulder, eager to get started. Her phone vibrated in her bag, and she fought the urge to open it and read the text. It was probably something sweet from Sebastian. If she read it, she'd only miss him more.

"I think there's a conference room open. Let's go there so we can have a little privacy," Leslie whispered, as if the offices were swarming with editors dying to eavesdrop on them.

She followed Leslie down a long hallway lined with framed *Vogue* covers and spreads, trying not to think of the amazing

Christmas present Sebastian had gotten for her. It was a photograph of a tiny seaside town, in an antique silver frame. Sun-bleached white stone houses clung to the rocky landscape, their cheerful red roofs contrasting with the heartbreaking blue of the Mediterranean. "This is where my family's from in Italy," Sebastian had explained in a soft voice. "I'm going to take you there." It made Brett's knees weak just thinking about it.

"Soo . . ." Leslie trailed off. She'd been talking about her subway ride that morning, and Brett had only been half listening. Leslie pushed open the door of a glass-walled conference room with enormous leather chairs and a sleek long table. Brett imagined Anna Wintour herself sitting at the head of the table and watching critically as her minions presented their layouts for her approval. "There's been a little, well, change in plans."

Brett's eyes widened as she sank into the leather chair that Leslie indicated. "What kind of change in plans?" she managed to squeak out. Hopefully they weren't going to send her down to the janitorial staff or anything.

Leslie leaned her elbows on the table and took a deep breath. "Well, as you know, I was happy to take you on as an intern, because my last intern completely fucked me over and left me with a shitload of work to get done before Fashion Week."

"Yes, of course." Brett leaned forward as well. She didn't mind running for coffee or making photocopies or even licking envelopes—she just wanted to be at *Vogue*, to feel it all around her. Ever since she'd had her letter to the editor published in *Seventeen* magazine when she was twelve, she'd fantasized about seeing her name in print again. "And I'm happy to do anything."

"Yes, well." Leslie coughed. It almost looked like she was trying to keep herself from smiling. "I'm afraid I've just been offered a promotion this morning—one that involves my transfer to Italian *Vogue*. I'll be moving to Milan next week."

"Oh." Brett felt her face flush. She certainly couldn't hold that against Leslie—who wouldn't want to jump at the chance to live in Italy? "That's great, isn't it?"

The smile Leslie had been trying to hide took over her face. "Yes! I've been dying to work over there for years—Italian women are so glamorous. And the *men*!" Brett almost spoke up in agreement, but stopped herself. Sebastian was the sexiest guy she'd ever met. Then the pained expression returned to Leslie's pretty face. "But, as you see, that means . . . I don't need you anymore. And it was too late for me to call you and tell you not to come in today."

"Can't I help out someone else?" Brett sputtered, caught off guard. "Really, I'm happy to do anything." Even being a member of the janitorial staff didn't sound so bad anymore.

Leslie shook her head sadly, pressing her thin lips together so firmly, they almost disappeared. "I asked around, and unfortunately no one really wants a high school intern. No offense!" she added immediately. Brett was still too stunned to really take offense.

She tucked her flaming red hair behind her ears. Suddenly the whole month stretched out before her. She thought she'd be in New York, sleeping on the couch in her sister's SoHo loft, working at *Vogue*, spending her evenings at poetry readings or sneaking into clubs with her fake ID. Now she had nothing to do.

Except head back to Waverly. And to Sebastian, which was a consolation. But although cuddling with her hot boyfriend might keep her busy, somehow Brett didn't think she was going to get school credit for it.

A WAVERLY OWL SHOULD ALWAYS BE WELL VERSED IN BASIC SURVIVAL SKILLS.

"Are we there yet?" Brandon Buchanan asked, adjusting the red frame backpack he'd borrowed from the Waverly Outing Club higher on his shoulders. He'd been following his roommate, Heath Ferro, through the thick woods that surrounded the Waverly Academy campus for what seemed like hours. "We've got to be miles away by now."

Even beneath his black microfleece hat and Ray-Ban visors, Brandon could read Heath's look of disgust. "Dude, don't start with me."

Brandon sighed inwardly as he followed Heath through the deep snow, pushing bare tree branches out of his face. He'd just gotten back to campus that morning, after his flight from Switzerland was delayed because of a blizzard in the Alps. The ten days after Christmas had been the best of his life, and strangely enough, he had Heath to thank for it. After all, it was Heath who'd bought Brandon the plane ticket to Switzerland to see Hellie Dunderdorf, Professor Dunderdorf's gorgeous daughter. Brandon had met her over Thanksgiving break, and since then she was the only girl he could even think about. For once, Brandon hadn't even minded being at home for Christmas, with his bottle-blond stepmother and his annoying three-year-old half brothers. Because twenty-four hours later, he got to hold Hellie in his arms again, kissing her soft, slightly chapped lips. The rest of the trip flew by. The two of them walked hand in hand, exploring the gorgeous campus of Le Rosey, the exclusive boarding school she attended. Or they holed up in her tiny yellow-walled bedroom, keeping each other warm.

By the time Brandon got back to Waverly on Monday morning, jet-lagged but happy, he hadn't even thought about his Jan Plan proposal. So when Heath offered to let Brandon jump in on his Jan Plan camping trip, Brandon immediately agreed. He figured they'd spend one night in the woods, take some notes about how to start a fire, maybe make a video of themselves rubbing a couple of sticks together. They could flesh it out later with some research about the history of the Rhinecliff Woods or some drawings of oak trees. Brandon had even seen Heath stuff a few packs of freeze-dried astronaut ice cream into his pack. Brandon had always loved that stuff.

And he did have an ulterior motive for joining the trip. He was looking forward to the opportunity to let Heath know—casually, of course—that he was no longer his virginal room-mate. The years of Heath teasing Brandon over his sexual inexperience were over.

But as they hiked farther and farther from Waverly's campus, the gray January sky began to turn purple. "Maybe we should set up camp now, you know?" Brandon said nervously. "It looks like it's going to snow."

Heath paused and shot Brandon an appraising look. "Not bad, Buchanan. Good eye. I scoped this spot out this morning." He pointed to a clump of white birch trees. They stood close together, as if huddling against the cold. "I already set up our camp."

"You did?" Brandon asked gratefully. He was exhausted and still jet-lagged. He just wanted to light a fire, take some notes for their paper, then curl up in his down-filled sleeping bag and pass out. "Where? I don't see our tent."

"Tent?" Heath smacked Brandon across the stomach with a branch he'd just cut with his machete-size Swiss Army knife. "Did you think we were going to spend three weeks in the wild sleeping in a fucking tent?"

Brandon dropped his pack to the ground. *"Three weeks?* What the hell are you talking about?" The sun dipped down behind the horizon, and Brandon felt his feet starting to numb. "I thought we were going to spend a night or two out here and record what we ate and shit. I brought my camera to take some pictures to supplement the paper."

Heath set his sack down on the back of a large boulder. "Dude, I bought you that plane ticket to Switzerland so you could fucking learn how to man up. Apparently, it didn't work."

"This has nothing to do with manning up." Brandon stared

at Heath, wondering if he had finally, literally, lost his mind. "We just can't live out in the snow for three weeks. And are you trying to say there's no tent?" Brandon noticed for the first time that the birch trees he'd seen had actually been chopped down and were strapped together with some kind of twine. They were leaning against the boulder to form a crude lean-to.

Carefully, Heath laid the evergreen boughs on the bare ground beneath the birches before turning to Brandon. "Haven't you ever seen *Man vs. Wild*?"

Brandon pressed his gloves to his eyes. He was exhausted, and Heath was trying to be some kind of Discovery Channel hero? "Heath, that's the shittiest shelter I've ever seen. We'll freeze to death."

"I watched three entire seasons of *Man vs. Wild* over break, and that dude does not bring a fucking tent. He doesn't have hot cocoa or goose-down pillows. He drinks his own piss if he has to." Heath pounded his fists against his chest like King Kong. "Besides, that shelter is way better than anything *you* could make."

Brandon inhaled the cold, pine-scented air and tried to get a grip. Whistling off-key, Heath gathered together a small bundle of sticks and set about constructing a fire. Brandon had to admit, his roommate kind of looked like he knew what he was doing.

But then Brandon poked his head inside the lean-to—which was easy, since there was no door. "Anything could just . . . walk right in." It was about one degree warmer than being in the open air. "And there's not exactly room for two people."

"Chill out, dude. It's supposed to be small to keep the body heat in. It's fucking cold out here."

Brandon groaned, too exhausted to fight. The jet lag was killing him. After he took a nap, he'd convince Heath to head back to campus and watch some more episodes of *Man vs. Wild* in the comfort of the Richards Hall common room instead.

He unrolled his sleeping bag, which felt perilously thin, and lay down on the lumpy evergreen boughs inside the lean-to. He started to doze off while Heath busied himself around the fire. Brandon was dreaming of Hellie, of being curled up next to her in her white cotton short shorts under her covers, when the acrid smell of burnt flesh reached his nose. With a start, he sat up and moved out of the lean-to. Heath was crouched over the fire, holding a long stick with a piece of meat on it.

"What the fuck is that?" Brandon tried to ask, but his face was numb. He slapped his cheeks, hoping he didn't have frostbite, and moved toward the fire. When he looked up at the sky, he saw fat flakes of snow falling.

"Meat is meat," Heath said with a devilish grin on his face, which looked strangely frozen, like the Joker's in *Batman*. "Don't ask where it came from—just enjoy!" He held the spear out to Brandon. On it was the scrawny red body of a freshly skinned squirrel.

Brandon's stomach lurched. "That can't be the only food we have." Brandon turned away, rubbing his hands over the fire. "Where are the provisions?"

"Those are for emergencies, dumbass." Heath brought the

stinky piece of meat to his mouth and took a tiny bite. "Mmm, tastes like chicken!"

Brandon got to his feet, which were also alarmingly numb. "This is not going to work." The fire was dying, and it was still fucking cold. His shoulder hurt from leaning against the boulder in the lean-to, where there wasn't actually enough room to stretch out fully. He wasn't about to cuddle up with Heath in there. "It's, like, negative twelve degrees out and I can already feel my organs starting to freeze." His stomach rumbled. "And I'm not eating anything that you catch."

Heath stood up as well. "Suck it up, pussy. It's supposed to stay above zero—for tonight, at least."

Brandon rubbed his hand on his forehead, which felt like an icebox. "Don't be an idiot. We can't stay out here in these conditions, sleeping on the ground under a couple of tied-together tree trunks. We'll freeze to death!"

"Dude, Bear Grylls survived Iceland! The Alaskan Range! The Andes—and let me tell you, the conditions were a fuck of a lot worse than these."

Brandon shook his head slowly. "Come on. Let's go back to campus. We'll go on some kind of special survivor hike out in the woods tomorrow—but seriously, we're going to die if we stay out in this tonight." And the thought of dying out here and never seeing Hellie again seemed like the worst thing on earth to Brandon at that moment.

Heath parked himself down in front of the fire and took another bite of squirrel meat. "I'm staying, man."

Brandon stared. Heath had that same determined look that

crossed his face every time he needed to prove some obnoxious point. "Fine, I'll let you keep my sleeping bag. You'll need it."

Heath scoffed, licking his fingers. "I don't even need mine."

"If you're not back in two days, I'll send out a search party." Brandon pulled his cell phone out of his pocket and checked for reception. The next best thing to having Hellie waiting for him when he got back to his room was a steaming-hot deep-dish pizza from Ritoli's.

And at least he was man enough to admit it.

RyanReynolds: Hey, sexy. Have a nice break?

AlisonQuentin: Eh. Good to be back, as always.

RyanReynolds: U going to the party in the basement of Maxwell tonight?

AlisonQuentin: Wouldn't miss it. Someone should invite the Dresden kids, no?

RyanReynolds: The girl, at least. I don't like the looks of that dude.

AlisonQuentin: What don't you like? He's hot.

RyanReynolds: Yeah, that's the problem.

WildernessMan Log: Heath vs. Wild
By Heath Ferro

Day 1

Woke at dawn to scout woods. Found prime location for shelter and built lean-to with birch saplings using ivy vines and trusty titanium Rambo 5.0 Full Tang knife. Too bad no one could see me do it. Returned later to settle in for the night with BB, who quickly pussied out. No worries. HF needs no one.

Noon temp: 24 degrees F. Not so bad.

Food: Created a snare and caught first squirrel. Cooked him on a stick till he was nice and crispy. Found some dark brown mushrooms beneath the snow for a late-night snack. Nothing more satisfying than catching and eating your own food.

Warmth: Plenty of wood for the campfire. Pine needles on floor of the shelter provide plenty of cushion. Cold is invigorating!

Mood: Excellent. Head feels clear. About to fall asleep with a full belly under the stars after a long day of work. All those babies back on campus, curled up under their down comforters, don't know what they're missing.

5

A WAVERLY OWL CAN ALWAYS SPOT A KINDRED

SPIRIT.

"A little higher . . . a little more. Harder, please. . . . Oh, yes, that's it," Tinsley moaned.

"Do you have any idea how dirty that sounds?" Julian McCafferty took his hands off her shoulders midmassage. Tinsley was sitting backward in Julian's desk chair, staring out the darkened window, as he worked all the tension out of her shoulders, tight from an early-morning indoor tennis match. The soothing sounds of an old Death Cab for Cutie song emanated from his Bose SoundDock.

"Of course, sweetie," Tinsley replied, closing her eyes. She loved the feel of Julian's strong hands on her shoulders. "Why do you think I'm doing it?"

Tinsley had spent a relaxing, shopping-fueled Christmas in New York with her parents—her mom felt so guilty about abandoning Tinsley for Thanksgiving that they'd nearly maxed out her AmEx card on a Madison Avenue spree. But the high-light of her break was meeting up with Julian at the Carmi-chaels' town house in Lake Placid. They'd spent long days on the slopes, making out on the ski lifts and racing each other back down the mountain. Julian was an even better skier than Tinsley, which drove her crazy—in ways good and bad. They spent their evenings curling up together in front of the fire with a bottle of wine, or soaking in the outdoor hot tub, watch-ing the crystalline stars appear in the clear night sky.

Julian pressed his lips to the nape of Tinsley's neck for a quick kiss before flopping facedown on his bed. He was so tall that his toes almost hung off the end of the regulation extra-long twin bed. The bottoms of his Diesel corduroys were frayed beyond repair. His blondish-brown hair was sun streaked from the days on the sunny ski slopes, and it had grown so long that he could pull it into a ponytail, which Tinsley kept threatening to chop off. "Come on over here. It's your turn to be masseuse."

"That's not the worst idea you've ever had." Tinsley stepped toward him, eager to run her hands all over his lean, muscular body, when a noise outside caught her attention. A few hearty male voices were followed by a chorus of girly giggles. It was the first night of Jan Plan, and since no one really had to get up in the morning, it was notoriously one of the best party nights. "But do you think we should maybe make a social appearance tonight? There's something going on in Maxwell."

Julian pushed onto his elbow and gazed up at Tinsley. He wore a gray T-shirt with a picture of a monkey wearing a space helmet. "You really want to go?"

Tinsley sank down onto the edge of the bed. She did, but she sensed that Julian didn't. "I don't know."

"Well, we've got a whole month of parties to look forward to. I'd rather, you know, just be with you." Julian grabbed a lock of Tinsley's hair and twirled it around his finger, something he'd made a habit of recently.

Sweet. But a twinge of regret shot through her—she was Tinsley Carmichael, after all. Shouldn't she be out there, in the middle of all the action? She thought fondly of last Jan Plan, when she and Brett and Callie had thrown an exclusive First Night party in their oversize Dumbarton dorm room. It was black tie, and invitation only, and they drank only the best Shiraz from Ryan Reynolds's family's vineyards.

But then Julian sat up and put his hand on Tinsley's waist, right at the spot where her skinny black Earl jeans didn't quite meet her tissue-soft Alice + Olivia T-shirt, and for a moment she forgot all about the rest of the planet. She crawled onto his lap, propping the heels of her new black leather Stuart Weitzman boots onto his nightstand, thinking, only fleetingly, what a shame it was to have such hot new boots and no one to gaze at them enviously.

"You know what I was thinking about?" Julian whispered into her ear, his breath hot against her skin.

Tinsley sighed dramatically, staring up at the giant black-and-white poster of a young Bob Dylan on the wall above Julian's bed. "I can guess." Yes, it was going to be so nice to have a whole month of hanging out with Julian, no classes, no responsibilities. She was going to start on her Jan Plan project tomorrow. She'd gotten a fancy new HD Nikon digital SLR camcorder from her father, and she'd been hoping to put together some kind of documentary. Over the summer, after she'd been—temporarily, it turned out—expelled from Waverly, she'd worked with her dad on a documentary about South Africa. Being behind the camera made Tinsley feel creative and powerful. Waverly Academy was, of course, not as exciting as Capetown, but she felt like she could make it work.

"Listen." Julian brushed a lock of Tinsley's dark hair behind her ear, then kissed her earlobe. "I know you're going to make a film for your Jan Plan, and I was talking to Alan St. Girard and a couple of the guys at lunch. We're going to try and write a kind of noir boarding-school mystery—you know, kind of Raymond Chandler meets *Carrie*."

"That's such a great idea!" Tinsley exclaimed, tracing her finger along Julian's jawbone. "You're the one who thought of it, I'm sure." She always forgot that Julian was just a freshman—he was so much smarter than any of the boys she knew when she was a freshman.

He shrugged modestly. "What can I say?"

Tinsley patted his cheek. "I'm pretty sure Heath Ferro's Jan Plan freshman year involved interviewing all the girls at Waverly and asking what made them horny."

"That's not a terrible idea, either." Julian grinned, a tiny dimple appearing beneath the corner of his lips. "But hey, you should work with us on the film. We'll need a femme fatale, and you could teach us all about directing and setting up shots."

"I'm flattered," Tinsley said slowly. She slid off his lap and sat next to him. "Maybe."

Julian tilted his head. "I promise I'll try to keep them from hitting on you too much, if that's what you're worried about."

"That's not it." Tinsley stood up. She couldn't very well tell Julian that it felt like a little *too* much to work on a school project with him—after all, they spent all their time together already. Suddenly Tinsley felt the need for some fresh air. She stretched her arms and grabbed her coat. "Listen, I'm going to run outside and have a cigarette, okay? I'll be right back."

She pulled on her brown wool herringbone Joie coat and tightened the belt. It was visitation hours, so girls were allowed in the boys' dorm, but doors were supposed to stay open. According to the ancient Waverly handbook, which read like a fussy girls' finishing-school manual from the 1800s, three feet had to be on the floor at all times in mixed company.

"Hurry back."

Tinsley rushed outside, grateful for the cool burst of air against her skin. She hadn't realized how warm it was inside Julian's room until she was out in the dark evening. She pulled the half-crushed pack of American Spirits from her coat pocket and stuck one between her lips, automatically glancing around for teachers. She stuck to the shadows of Wolcott Hall, trying not to step in any mud. In the distance, she saw a couple of girls hurrying across the quad. In their impractically short skirts and high heels, they were clearly on their way to a party.

Tinsley wandered around the corner of the building, letting the cigarette smoke seep into her lungs and relax her. There, sitting on a bench directly under one of the iron gas lamps that lined the campus paths, was a girl in a short black jacket with a fur-trimmed hood. A cigarette casually dangled from her lips. Tinsley blinked. Lots of people smoked at Waverly, but no one wanted to get caught doing it. And this girl wasn't exactly hiding it.

Then she realized. It was the girl from the chapel stage—the dean's daughter. A worn-looking gray cap was perched haphazardly on her head, and her wild dark hair peeked out from beneath it.

The girl looked up. "Hey," she said, coolly, taking another puff of a cigarette. Tinsley casually dropped her own cigarette butt to the ground and stamped it out with her toe before walking over to the girl.

"Do you always lurk around in the dark?"

"Only when I'm doing something I shouldn't be doing." Tinsley stuffed her gloved hands into her pockets. "But I see *you* don't have the same healthy fear of authority."

"When your daddy's the dean, you develop warped ideas of what authority is." The girl laughed. Her heart-shaped face was pale and surprisingly innocent looking. "Nice boots."

Immediately, Tinsley felt vindicated. Her boots were just waiting to be appreciated. "Thanks."

"I'm Isla," the girl replied, crossing her legs. She wore a red wool miniskirt, black leggings, and a pair of knee-high Doc Martens.

"Tinsley Carmichael," Tinsley replied.

Isla's sea green eyes widened, and she leaned forward. A woven copper ring on her right index finger caught Tinsley's eye. "I was *wondering* when I'd meet the famous Tinsley Carmichael. I've heard a lot about you."

Tinsley laughed lightly, but of course she was flattered by the recognition of her own notoriety. "Don't believe it all."

"That's a shame. I thought there were going to be some cool people here." Isla arched one of her thin eyebrows and took another drag of her cigarette. "Don't worry," she said as she caught Tinsley's eyes on the unconcealed cigarette, "one of the perks of being the dean's daughter is that it's nearly impossible to get in trouble."

Tinsley sat down next to her on the bench. The cold quickly seeped through her jeans, but she didn't care. "What are the other perks?"

Isla laughed, one of those loud, carefree, completely infectious laughs. "Have you ever been inside the dean's house here? It is fucking sweet." Isla's wide eyes made her look slightly wild—probably an accurate assessment.

"I have, actually," Tinsley admitted proudly, rubbing her arms with her leather-gloved hands. "Once, as a freshman, this guy and I snuck in. It was a weekend Marymount was away, and we raided the wine cellar."

Isla nodded, impressed. "Nice." She got to her feet and flicked her cigarette butt into the snow, where it sizzled out. She straightened her cropped leather jacket. "Any other exciting hiding places on campus?"

Tinsley grinned and rubbed her hands together, thinking of the times she and Julian sneaked into the Cinephiles screening room to make out. "I just met you. I can't tell you all my secrets."

Isla threw her head back and let out a long laugh that echoed through the quiet night. "Tinsley Carmichael," she said slowly, lighting another cigarette and taking a long drag. "I think this is the beginning of a beautiful friendship."

OwlNet

From: BrandonBuchanan@waverly.edu
To: MarielPritchard@waverly.edu
Date: Monday, January 3, 9:15 P.M.
Subject: Jan Plan

Ms. Pritchard,

I know I handed in my Jan Plan proposal this afternoon to do an
"outdoor survival" project with Heath Ferro, but after thoughtful
consideration I realized I might be better suited to a different project.
I know that tomorrow is the deadline for proposals. Is it all right if I
e-mail you in the afternoon?

Thank you,

Brandon

 **Owl Net**

From: MarielPritchard@waverly.edu
To: BrandonBuchanan@waverly.edu
Date: Monday, January 3, 10:24 P.M.
Subject: Re: Jan Plan

Brandon,

Don't worry too much—I wasn't convinced the "Survivor" project
was really up your alley. I do need your new proposal by 5:00 pm
tomorrow, so please make haste. If it helps, one of my other advisees,
Callie Vernon, is working alone on a project that could probably use two
people, in case you'd like to get in touch with her.

Look forward to reading your proposal!

Best,

MP

6

A WAVERLY OWL KNOWS THAT IT ALWAYS HELPS TO

HAVE AN ALLY.

Bright and early on Tuesday morning, Jenny let the front door to Stansfield Hall slam behind her as she headed toward the dean's office. As suspected, her adviser, Ms. Rose, had told her she needed to get permission directly from the dean if she wanted to work on her own. Now she just needed to convince him she was justified.

The administrative building was silent except for the muffled sound of music and the hissing of the old metal radiators. The wet bottoms of Jenny's dark green Wellies squeaked against the waxed wooden floors. For the first time, she wondered if teachers appreciated Jan Plan as much as students. After all, they didn't really have to teach classes, just look in on their advisees and occasionally lead an independent study. *Did teachers have their own parties?* she suddenly wondered, trying to picture Ms. Rose standing around a keg with the anal Latin teacher, Mr. Gaston. Or doing body shots. Ew.

Shaking that disturbing image from her mind, she marched toward the new dean's door. Mr. Tompkins, Marymount's secretary, was not at his desk—in fact, it was empty except for a Waverly pencil cup and a flat desk calendar. When a dean left, did that mean their secretary had to leave, too? Like with a presidential administration? *Guess I just go and introduce myself*, Jenny thought, butterflies fluttering in her stomach. She glanced at herself in the reflection of the large, café-style mirror that hung in the waiting area. She'd chosen her black three-quarter-sleeve Banana Republic top and a pair of Seven jeans she'd found at a thrift store years ago and loved to paint in. The paint splatters, she hoped, would make her seem serious about her art project.

Just as she raised her hand to knock on the door, it flung open. Jenny leaped back in surprise—and so did Dean Dresden. "Oh! Hello there." He stepped back, dropping a stack of brightly colored paint samples to the floor.

"I'm so sorry to interrupt," Jenny blurted out, bending down to pick up a handful of the small squares of paper. The office was a huge room with enormous bay windows that looked out over the quad. Over the outstretched bare branches of the trees, a tiny glimpse of the blue-gray Hudson River was visible in the distance. "I can come back if this is a bad time."

"No, no." The dean grinned, grabbing the rest of the samples from the floor. "My wife's just been hounding me to change the color of the office before I get completely settled. So excuse the mess. And please come in."

"She doesn't like . . . beige?" Jenny asked, stepping into the office after him. She'd only had to meet with Dean Marymount once, but it was still strange to see his office almost completely emptied out. The only furniture was a big oak desk and two large armchairs, one of which was set behind the desk. The walls—painted a bland color that made Jenny think of a doctor's office—were completely bare save for the nails where Dean Marymount's various pictures used to hang. A stack of white cardboard boxes stood in the corner.

The new dean's face turned expectantly toward her.

"I guess it does look a bit . . . blah."

"That's exactly what she said." Dean Dresden shook his head as he tossed the samples down on his desk and extended his hand out to Jenny. "Anyway. I'm Dean Dresden. And I'm always happy to meet one of my new students."

"I'm Jenny Humphrey." Jenny smiled, feeling the butterflies in her stomach start to settle down. "I'm a sophomore, but this is my first year at Waverly, too."

"A fellow newbie." Dean Dresden laughed, sliding into his chair. "Well, tell me, Jenny Humphrey, what can I do for you today?"

Jenny sank into the chair opposite the desk. "I wanted to ask if it would be possible for me to do an independent project this Jan Plan."

For the first time since she walked in, the smile left the dean's lips, even though his eyes kept smiling. "May I ask why? It's your first Jan Plan, after all. The administration designed the program so that students would learn to work together in teams."

"I realize that." Jenny gave him what she hoped was a winning smile, even though her dad called it her Little Orphan Annie smile. "But it's about exploring something you're passionate about, too, right?"

The dean nodded thoughtfully. "I suppose that's part of it as well."

"Well, throughout the fall semester, my art classes played an important part in keeping me grounded." Jenny paused. She knew she sounded like a suck-up. She tried again. "I just feel like I had so much to absorb that it would be really great for me to try and process all that information right now. I had two art classes with Mrs. Silver—portraiture and advanced figure drawing. And they were great. But I started to think about what it would be like to draw people in motion . . . almost as if I were a camera whose shutter was kept open while it was taking a picture."

"I have to admit—I'm impressed that you even know how a manual camera works," the dean laughed.

Jenny took the laughter as a good sign and leaned forward in her chair. "I want to try to imagine slowing down the movements and capturing them at each moment. I'd love to study people in all kinds of situations—just walking, or dancing, or maybe skiing. And I just think this is the sort of project I'd have to work on independently."

The dean nodded and frowned simultaneously, and Jenny's heart sank. "I can see your point, but unfortunately you're a sophomore. And rules are rules. Maybe next year you can work on this."

Jenny, who'd felt so comfortable at the start of this meeting, could feel her lip tremble. She was always nervous around authority figures—and right now it took a lot of willpower to keep a tear from trickling down her face.

"Hey, Dad."

Both Jenny and the dean whirled their heads toward the open door. "Oh, sorry." Standing in the door frame was the handsome dark-haired boy who'd sat onstage at the chapel meeting. He wore a thick navy blue sweater and a pair of khakis with frayed hems. He looked like a perfect prep-school boy—with a possibly devilish gleam in his eyes. "I didn't realize you were in a meeting. Mom told me you forgot your BlackBerry."

The boy's piercing green eyes focused on Jenny, making her feel an entirely different kind of nervous. Had he barged in . . . on purpose? Jenny shifted in her seat, grateful that she had taken the time to twist her hair into two loose, arty braids. She blew an escaped curl out of her eyes.

The dean patted the front pocket of his shirt absentmindedly. "Jenny Humphrey, this is my son, Isaac. Jenny was just pitching me a Jan Plan project."

Isaac came forward and handed his dad the BlackBerry, then sat on the corner of the desk, as if he were in no hurry to leave. "Really?" His eyes flicked to his father. "Can I hear about it?"

The dean gestured toward Jenny to go ahead. Her stomach flip-flopped. It was nerve-racking enough to try and explain her idea to the dean—now she had to do it in front of his gorgeous son, too? After taking a deep breath, she explained her project once again, trying to keep her cheeks from blushing.

"That sounds awesome," Isaac said when she was done. "Good luck with that."

Dean Dresden shifted uncomfortably in his chair. "Unfortunately, it will have to wait until next year, as Jenny is a sophomore."

Isaac glanced at Jenny, a slightly quizzical look on his face. "And I'm a junior. Why does it matter?"

Dean Dresden smiled patiently at his son. "Because sophomores have to work in pairs or small groups."

"But juniors and seniors don't? That's a weird rule." Isaac rubbed his chin thoughtfully. "That's a shame. It seems like Waverly would *want* its students to be creative."

Dean Dresden frowned. "Isaac, I'm not sure this is the right time for this."

"Sorry, Dad." He crossed his arms in front of him and glanced at Jenny. "I just think that a lot of schools are so regimented, they crush creativity. And we just landed in one that ostensibly encourages it—except, for some reason, not for sophomores or freshmen." He got to his feet and wandered over to the almost-empty bookcase, where he picked up a prism-shaped paperweight and passed it back and forth between his palms. "Just seems weird."

The dean wiped his hand across his face and turned to Jenny. "Jenny, what do you have to say? Besides that my son is destined for a profession in law?"

Jenny felt her entire face turn red. "I'd say that . . . yes, I agree with Isaac." She glanced at him and felt her face turn even hotter. "I think it's really important to be able to explore our artistic interests. I'd really love the chance to do this on my own."

"All right, I give up." The dean cleared his throat. "An artist is an artist. I'll send an e-mail to your adviser and let her know I've approved you for an independent project. But before you go . . ."

Jenny's heart dropped. She exchanged another glance with Isaac but had to pull her eyes away quickly. His eyes were like quicksand, and she didn't want to get caught staring at him in front of the dean. "Yes?"

The dean grabbed two of the paint samples from his desk and held them up for Jenny to see. "Put your artistic eyes on these. Which do you think is a better color for this room?"

Jenny bit her lip to keep from smiling and scratched her head as she made her best deep-in-thought face. "I'd say the sunflower yellow. It would look nice with the dark wood. And it'll make everyone happy to be in here."

The dean nodded. "That's what I thought, too. Not that my presence isn't cheerful enough." He smiled again. "I look forward to seeing your project at the end of Jan Plan. I hope it'll be worth the wait."

Jenny mumbled something in reply as the dean walked her to the door. Over his shoulder, she caught a glimpse of Isaac's electric eyes watching her. "Nice to meet you," she said, trying to say "thank you" with her eyes.

Isaac gave a slight smile. "You, too."

A chill ran down her spine as Jenny turned and marched through the empty foyer. She felt like she was floating on air, the whole glorious month stretching out in front of her like a blank canvas. She was glad she'd taken the chance of asking for the dean's permission. He wasn't as intimidating as she'd thought.

And his son was even cuter close-up.

 **OwlNet**

BennyCunningham: People are hanging out in Richards's basement tonight. You coming?

TinsleyCarmichael: I hadn't heard about it.

BennyCunningham: That's because you and your husband are too busy cuddling to party!

TinsleyCarmichael: Jealousy is unattractive, Benny. You'll find a boyfriend someday.

BennyCunningham: Don't be a bitch! U know we just miss you. Come out!

TinsleyCarmichael: I'll think about it.

A FRIEND OF A BOYFRIEND IS A FRIEND OF AN OWL.

Brett tightened her cropped Anna Sui military jacket around her as she squeezed past a pair of tank-size strollers outside CoffeeRoasters, the tiny coffee shop in downtown Rhinecliff, on Tuesday morning. She pushed the glass door open and stepped into the humid café, trying not to compare the dingy coffee shop to the cute SoHo bistros where she could have been breakfasting. She'd gotten back to Waverly that morning and was still a little out of sorts. She loved school; she really did. But she was supposed to be spending her January hanging out at NYC hot spots like the Waverly *Inn*—not the Waverly library.

Then she caught sight of Sebastian, reading on a velvet couch in the back of the crowded café. A little jolt spread from her cold cheeks down to the toes of her slouchy, distressed leather boots. He was so engrossed in his copy of *On the Road* that he didn't notice her approach.

"Nice to see you again, too." Brett nudged her toe into Sebastian's leg when he didn't look up.

Sebastian's face lit up when he saw her. He jumped to his feet. "Thought you were taking the later train back." He leaned toward her, his dark brown eyes jubilant, and pressed his mouth to her cheek. "I would've picked you up at the station."

Brett shrugged. She'd taken a cab to campus because she was still bent out of shape about her *Vogue* internship falling through and wanted the extra time alone. But now, with Sebastian in front of her, looking sexy in his plain black American Apparel T-shirt, it was hard to imagine being anywhere else. "I knew you'd just try to get me to come back to your room and make out."

A faux hurt look crossed Sebastian's face. "And there's something wrong with that?" He stroked Brett's arm.

"*Yes.*" Brett threw herself down onto the couch, letting her giant Diesel duffel bag land on the wet floor. "Today's the deadline for Jan Plan proposals, and I'm suddenly without a project."

"So if I help you figure out what to do, then we can go back to my room?" He raised his dark eyebrows expectantly.

Brett rolled her eyes but was secretly pleased. "I guess."

"Good." Sebastian sat back down on the couch and crossed his arms across his chest. "Because I have an idea."

"If it's going to involve me posing on the hoods of various muscle cars, I don't think it'll work."

Sebastian pretended to consider the idea, then laughed. "I know a girl who's doing a fashion project, and the partner she had lined up bailed on her. Do you know Christine Bosley? Chrissy?"

Brett raised her eyebrows. Chrissy was one of the theater kids, but one of the more normal ones. A tall, gangly girl who always wore really elaborate necklaces. "What kind of fashion project?"

"Got me. Something about costumes." Sebastian took a sip of his coffee. "I just heard her complaining about all the work she had to do in the mailroom."

Brett took a deep breath. Chrissy had always seemed nice enough, and Brett was pretty desperate. She needed to have something to show Mrs. Horniman, her adviser, by five. Quickly, she fumbled for her Nokia and rattled off a short e-mail to ChristineBosley@waverly.edu.

"Now, come here." Sebastian patted the spot next to him on the sofa, and Brett slid over till she was almost in his lap. She let her head fall against his chest. He smelled like cappuccino and cinnamon toothpaste.

Maybe Jan Plan at Waverly wouldn't be so bad after all.

Later that afternoon, Brett strode across campus toward Merritt House, a gray clapboard building with an enormous front porch. It used to be faculty housing but had been converted to student housing in the eighties. All the rooms had private baths. Now it was where most of the arty music and theater girls ended up. It was at the far end of the snow-covered quad, which was pulsing with activity. A snow sculpture competition was going on, and Owls were running around with buckets of snow and water and various sharp tools that looked like they should be used for gardening. Brett spotted the Disciplinary Committee adviser, Mr. Wilde, helping a group of freshman guys build what looked like a giant Snoopy.

Brett climbed the creaky steps and followed the directions to Chrissy's room on the third floor. The door to room 3D was covered with a stage poster of *Cabaret*. Brett knocked, and almost instantly the door was opened by a tall girl with a sleek platinum bob. She wore a pair of black leggings and a black-and-white striped off-the-shoulder T-shirt dress that hugged her slim, dancerlike body. She grinned at Brett. "Hey, Brett. Come on in!"

"I really appreciate you letting me latch onto your project, Chrissy." Brett stepped into the room, a tiny, brightly lit single with its bed pushed under the lowest part of the sloping attic ceiling. The floor was completely covered with pictures from magazines and art prints and random objects, like a jeweled ladybug brooch and a piece of paisley tablecloth. It looked like someone's junk drawer had exploded all over the floor. "My project fell through unexpectedly," she explained.

"Don't mention it. I could totally use the help." Chrissy shrugged. She had an acorn-shaped beauty mark on her left shoulder. "I think I got overly ambitious. I somehow volunteered to design *and* make all the costumes for the spring musical."

"That sounds like a lot of work. But awesome, too," Brett said, getting excited. Instead of writing copy about the same old designers who had been around forever, here was the opportunity to actually work on the designs. Who needed *Vogue*? "How did you manage that?"

"Mr. Shepard's my adviser—and he totally loves me." Mr. Shepard was the long-haired, reportedly pot-smoking head of the theater department. He'd been a Vietnam War protester who'd dodged the draft by sneaking over the Canadian border and starting a hippie commune in British Columbia. "I was the costume designer for *1984* last year."

"Wait, wasn't that the show where everyone wore Saran Wrap?" The whole cast had appeared before the DC for indecent exposure after some visiting parents had complained, but they'd decided to dismiss the charges. Brett hung her coat over the back of Chrissy's chair and knelt on the floor to get a better look at the scraps.

Chrissy nodded gleefully, casually flopping herself down on the floor and crossing her legs, Buddha-style. "You would *not* believe how many boxes of that stuff we had to go through, just so the actors wouldn't be, you know. X-rated."

Brett giggled. "I hope you're not looking to top that with this?"

"No. Shep said I had to keep it PG this time." Chrissy rubbed her hands together excitedly. "We're doing *Les Mis*."

"Really?" Brett's eyes lit up. She'd read *Les Misérables* last year in Madame Renault's class, and it was wildly romantic—in that French, completely heart-shattering way. "Nineteenth-century French fashion? How fun."

"Yes, completely." Chrissy clapped her hands, her blond hair falling across her forehead. It was refreshing to be in the presence of someone else whose hair color was a shade that did not appear in nature, Brett thought as she tucked her stop-sign-red hair behind her ears. Maybe she needed to hang out with theater girls more often. "It's going to rock!"

"So, that's what all this stuff is for?" Brett asked, picking up a thick art history book covered with bright orange Post-it notes. Edith Piaf was playing softly on the stereo. When Chrissy did something, she really got into it. "Inspiration?"

Chrissy nodded, snatching up a black-and-white photograph of a Parisian street crowded with horse-drawn carriages. "I've sort of grabbed everything I could get my hands on at the library. French art, French history."

Brett held up a copy of Julia Child's *Mastering the Art of French Cooking*. "French food?"

"Okay, I don't know what I was thinking with that one." Chrissy laughed, fumbling through the pictures on the floor. "I had this postcard of the *Venus de Milo*. Where'd it go?"

Brett stood up, noticing some postcards thumbtacked onto the bulletin board above Chrissy's desk. "She's naked, isn't she? I hope you're not getting more ideas," Brett giggled. She'd forgotten how nice it was to work on something creative. This was kind of what she imagined her *Vogue* internship would be like, minus the sitting-on-the-floor part.

"Here it is." Brett plucked the postcard of the *Venus de Milo* statue from the board. She was about to turn back to Chrissy when something else caught her eye. A postcard of a tiny coastal Italian village, brilliant white buildings covered in jumbles of red tiles. Brett squinted. It looked like the same town in the photograph Sebastian had given her for Christmas—the village where his grandmother lived on the Amalfi Coast. Sebastian's family spent three weeks every summer there. Had he sent Chrissy a postcard?

That was . . . sweet. But also a little odd. Did boys really send friends postcards?

"What do think about a sort of sixties retro, boho-peasant look? You know, revamped a little?" Chrissy asked, chewing on the end of a pink Hello Kitty pencil. "Sort of like Nicole Richie meets . . . *Hunchback of Notre Dame.*"

"I think it could work," Brett answered, absentmindedly. She was sure that at some point in her lifetime she'd sent a platonic male friend a postcard. Hadn't she mailed Brandon Buchanan a postcard of the Parthenon from Athens one summer? It was just a nice way to keep in touch. "But maybe I should have told you sooner, I don't know anything about sewing."

"I'll teach you." Chrissy laughed, ruffling her hair with her left hand. "It's easier than you think."

Brett smiled back. Okay, she liked Chrissy. Besides, any friend of Sebastian's was a friend of hers.

Right?

OwlNet

JulianMcCafferty:	Miss you.
TinsleyCarmichael:	U R sweet.
JulianMcCafferty	Just took *The Third Man* out from the lib. Wanna watch tonight?
TinsleyCarmichael:	Maybe . . . Thought I might stop in at the party in Richards' basement. U in?
JulianMcCafferty:	I kinda feel like doing some research for the script.
TinsleyCarmichael:	Oh. OK. Maybe I'll stop by after.

**A WAVERLY OWL KNOWS THAT THE FUTURE IS
MUCH MORE INTERESTING THAN THE PAST.**

Callie peeked around the open door of the rare books
library on Tuesday afternoon. She was ostensibly looking for a quiet place to prepare her ideas for her psychology project, but in reality, she was just drawn to this room.
It was a beautiful space—a second-floor balcony with a polished mahogany railing looked out over the distressed leather
armchairs and glass-doored bookcases below. Glass-covered
display tables offered up rare editions of leather-bound manu-
scripts, and diffuse light filtered in through the tall, curtained
windows. It was almost always empty save for Mr. Gruber, the
rare books librarian, who stayed in his second-floor office and
fawned over the recently acquired first folio of Shakespeare with
white gloves.

But Callie wasn't exactly interested in the books. She loved
the rare books library because it was the first place Easy Walsh

had kissed her. Even though they'd broken up, she couldn't stop thinking about him. And she didn't really want to.

Callie rubbed her arms and sank into a leather loveseat. Mr. Gruber claimed he maintained the sixty-degree temperature for the sake of the books, but Callie suspected he didn't want students lingering in his private lair. (She hoped he didn't do anything too weird in there.) At least she'd come prepared, wearing her coziest Juicy Couture cashmere lounge pants and hoodie. A couple of Dumbarton girls had thrown an appletini party in the upstairs common room last night, and Callie was still a little hungover. It was nice to be alone to brood.

"Callie. You've got to let me work with you."

Callie cringed when she heard a male voice. She looked like crap today. But she realized with relief that it was only Brandon Buchanan. Even though they'd dated all of freshman year, she didn't quite think of him as a *guy*. He had nicer clothes than she did, his skin was always perfectly moisturized, and he was just a little too *neat*.

Except . . . he looked kind of scruffy today. Stubble covered his chin, and his golden brown hair stood up a little wildly, as if he hadn't showered yet.

"What are you talking about?" Callie demanded crossly, closing the leather notebook where she'd been doodling instead of working. "Why would you want to work with me? And I don't *have* to do anything." Ms. Emory had rubber-stamped her proposal to work alone, which suited Callie just fine.

"I didn't mean to say it like that," Brandon said sheepishly, running a hand through his hair. His rumpled Ben Sherman button-down looked like he'd slept in it. "Sorry."

"What's *with* you?" Callie turned her back to him and pretended to look at her notebook. She grabbed her tube of Smashbox lip gloss and spread some on her lips. "I thought you were doing some camping thing with Heath."

"Yeah, well." Brandon headed toward one of the display tables and touched the edge of an old copy of *Charlotte's Web*. "Turns out Heath's *insane*—imagine that. And since I value my life, I thought I'd be safer doing a different project." He glanced over his shoulder. "Pritchard said you were working alone, so I kind of hoped I could butt in and help you."

Callie eyed Brandon. Something about him was different, and it wasn't just the beard scruff and the wrinkled shirt. She hadn't talked to him in ages, but she'd heard that he'd spent his Christmas vacation hooking up with one of Professor Dunderdorf's hot daughters in Switzerland, having sex nonstop. She hadn't believed it at the time—Brandon practically had a scarlet *V*, for *Virgin*, branded onto his forehead. But now he seemed *different*, somehow. Maybe it *was* true.

"Fine," she said at last. It could be kind of fun to work with Brandon. He was always polite, and he could be counted on to do the boring things, like typing up notes or putting together a bibliography. "Basically, I just want to explore the idea of what love is—and try and figure out if true love is a real thing, or if it's like some kind of security blanket. . . ."

"And let me guess, you're going to find that out by interviewing a bunch of your friends—girls who think true love is what they feel for Prada?" Brandon asked incredulously, chuckling a little as he crossed his arms over his chest.

"Hey!" Callie shot him an evil look. Since when was Brandon so cocky? "If you don't like my project, you can go back to the woods with Heath." She stuck her tongue out at him.

Brandon held his hands up defensively. "You're right. I'm totally at your mercy. And, honestly, I think it's a cool topic. Really."

Callie sniffed. She unzipped her Prada bag, feeling slightly self-conscious, and thrust a sheet of paper at him. "The interviewing is only going to be part of the project, anyway. The rest is research on the psychology and chemistry of love. But here's my question list, if you're interested." She flicked open her phone and glanced at the time. She didn't know why, but she wanted Brandon to know she had better things to be doing than talking to him. Even though she didn't.

"*Do you believe in love at first sight?*" Brandon read off, a funny grin on his face. "*Or do you just want to believe in it?*" Brandon looked up at Callie, who felt herself blushing. She kind of wished she'd taken the time to throw on some less-frumpy clothes. Not that she cared what Brandon thought, but just to seem a little more professional. Normally, he'd be drooling all over her. Instead, he was looking at her with that slightly bored, amused look in his eyes.

"We're supposed to be asking the subjects, Brandon, not each other." Callie rolled her eyes. But as her eyes fell on Brandon's smirking face, she had a thought: this was where he'd walked in on her making out with Easy Walsh sophomore year, the night of the *Absinthe* lit mag party. She'd been dating Brandon all year, but all it took was one smoldering look from Easy that night, and she'd followed him into this very room. They'd kissed for what seemed like hours before Brandon, searching for his girlfriend, finally walked in on them. He was probably reliving that humiliation over and over again. No wonder he was acting weird.

Brandon opened his mouth to reply, when a loud buzzing stopped him. He fumbled in the pocket of his jacket for his phone. Was he taking a *call* after practically begging her to join her project? Glancing at the number, his face completely lit up. "Heyyyy," he said in a lowered voice, reflexively turning his back on Callie for some privacy. "I was just thinking about you."

Callie's jaw dropped. He was taking a call from his Swiss girlfriend? How rude. Quickly, Callie tried to look busy, shuffling through her papers and jotting down notes on the questions.

Brandon leaned his elbows on one of the glass display tables that housed a priceless medieval prayer book, something that would have given Mr. Gruber a heart attack. Tiny signs that read NO LEANING in florid cursive writing were taped all over the cases. "Nothing much. I'm just working with Callie on this project about love, interviewing people and stuff. . . . Callie? Yeah, but . . . that's ancient history." There was a pause, then he laughed. "Yes, exactly."

Callie dropped her notebook to the floor with a slap. She'd never felt more insulted. Since when did Brandon think of her as *ancient history*? It hadn't been that long ago that they dated. And she wasn't ancient *anything*.

Brandon held the phone to his ear with one hand as he casually ran his fingers across the parchment-colored globe in the center of the room. He had an annoying grin on his handsome face. As he spun the globe on its axis, the continents and oceans blurring together, Callie noticed the way his shirt tightened against his biceps. Had he been working out?

Irritated, she marched toward him and held out her wrist, angrily tapping at the spot where a watch would be if she wore one. An amused look crossed Brandon's face before he turned away again. "Look, Hellie, I've got to go. We're in the middle of something. I'll talk to you later, okay?" Reluctantly, he ended the call and slipped the phone back into his pocket.

"I need you to focus, Brandon, if you want to work with me on this." Callie was amazed at how bitchy she sounded. She took a deep breath.

"Yes, Captain." Brandon replied, giving her a mock salute. He smiled cheerfully, but for once his clear green eyes were totally devoid of the look of puppy-dog longing she was used to seeing there.

And somehow, it made him look even more handsome.

Callie shook her head clear. Was it the weird, oxygen-heavy air in here that was making her feel light-headed? Because she couldn't possibly be attracted to Brandon Buchanan again.

Could she?

 **OwlNet**

From: CallieVernon@waverly.edu
To: Women of Waverly list
Date: Tuesday, January 4, 9:15 P.M.
Subject: The Science of Love

Hey, Ladies!

Wanna help me out by participating in my Jan Plan project on LOVE?
I know everyone has an opinion on the topic. So, please join me to
answer some thoughtful questions tomorrow afternoon from 2–4 pm at
Reynolds Atrium. Snacks will be provided!

Thanks,

Callie

A WAVERLY OWL ISN'T AFRAID TO PLUNGE INTO A NEW PROJECT.

Tinsley pushed open the steamed-up door to the Waverly Athletic Club on Tuesday afternoon, her red canvas yoga bag slung over her shoulder. Mabel Moody, a senior Tinsley had taken Italian with, was teaching an Ashtanga yoga class as her Jan Plan project. *So* much better than calculus. Tinsley had a few hours before she had to e-mail her Jan Plan proposal to her adviser, and she planned to think it all through while in Downward-Facing Dog.

Tinsley flashed her ID card at the check-in desk. A senior jock named Bradley waved her through, barely glancing up from his iPhone screen. She strode across the lobby, heading for the girls' locker room just as the door to the boys' locker room swung open. Out sauntered Isla Dresden. She wore a super-short black turtleneck dress and a pair of patterned tights. Her expression was nonchalant, as if exiting the boys' locker room was a normal Tuesday afternoon activity.

"Hey, what were you doing in there?" Bradley appeared next to Tinsley, a silver whistle around his neck. His burgundy polo shirt with the Waverly crest was two sizes too small. "That's the boys' locker room."

"I'm so sorry." Isla smiled sweetly, tousling her wet hair. Tinsley raised an eyebrow. Had she showered in there? "I'm new here."

"Oh, right." Unconsciously, Bradley kneaded his oversize bicep with his other hand. "Well, if you ever want a private tour . . ."

Isla pursed her curvy pink lips. "I'll keep that in mind." A crowd of students streamed through the front door, and Bradley reluctantly returned to his post at the front desk.

Tinsley, who'd been silent through the whole exchange, was about to scoot into the girls' locker room when Isla caught sight of her. Her eyes lit up. "Just the girl I've been looking for."

"Not in the boys' locker room, I hope." Tinsley was pleased Isla had sought her out. Normally, she was a little wary whenever a pretty new girl showed up on campus, but Isla seemed like she wanted to play nice. "I haven't been in there in ages."

"Nah." Isla lowered her voice. "I was just doing a little recon for my Jan Plan project. *That's* why I was looking for you, actually. I thought you might want to work with me."

Tinsley glanced at her watch. She was going to be late for the yoga class, but suddenly she didn't mind. "Okay, I'm intrigued."

"Look at this." Isla dropped her leather saddle bag on the glass-topped coffee table in the lobby and pulled out an over-size photography book. Tinsley followed her, stepping over an abandoned copy of *Men's Health*. "This is one of my favorite photographers. Look at the incredible things he does."

Tinsley watched as Isla flipped the pages. It was an amazing book of portraits, *Vogue*-style spreads that showed people in crazy, improbable scenes: a model wearing a bikini on a snow-covered mountain top, or a pair of outrageously high heels while running around a track. It was a study in contrast, mixing fashion with cool backgrounds and scenes from life. "This is gorgeous."

"Right?" Isla grabbed the book and held it open in front of her. "Imagine how *even more* gorgeous these pictures would be if the models were you and me. We should totally photograph each other, using this as inspiration."

Tinsley bit her lip. The full-page spreads were classy, museum-quality photographs. She could easily imagine herself in a white-walled art gallery, surrounded by giant reproductions of these photos—except, of course, with her as one of the models. "I don't know," Tinsley replied, at last. "I'm not sure it's exactly my thing."

In truth, Tinsley had always fantasized about being a model. Once, when she was eight, a modeling scout spotted her throwing bread to the ducks in the Central Park duck pond and pressed her card into Tinsley's mom's hand, begging her to call. But Tinsley's mother refused, insisting that it was more impor-tant for Tinsley to rely on her wits than her looks. So far, *both* had proven useful.

"Come on," Isla pleaded, snapping the photography book shut. "Think how many cool shoots we could do around campus. Maybe we could find some old wedding dresses and rappel down the side of the chapel in them." Isla's eyes sparkled with excitement. "You have to work with me. I can't do it alone."

For a moment, Tinsley thought of Julian. He'd asked her to work on his film with him, and she'd told him she'd think about it. It was a cool project and everything, but the last thing Tinsley wanted was to become one of those couples who never had any separate interests, who were content to lounge around together wearing nasty sweatpants all day. *Sweatpants couples.* It gave her nightmares. "Let's do it," she said, after a beat.

Isla's green eyes lit up. "Excellent. I've got my camera with me." She shook the Nikon bag hanging at her side. "Can you start now?"

A pack of senior guys in sweaty workout clothes came clattering out of the weight room. Tinsley felt their eyes fall on her and Isla. It was a good feeling. "Sure," she replied, tossing her hair. "Let's do it."

"I was hoping you'd say that." Isla fumbled through her bag for a second, her wavy dark hair falling in front of her face. She grabbed something bright red and tossed it to Tinsley. "Put this on."

"Are you crazy?" Tinsley giggled as she held the tiny string bikini up against her coat. She could already see Bradley staring at them from behind the counter. "Do you always carry a spare bikini with you?"

"I was a Girl Scout for three years before they kicked me

out." Isla shrugged. She hefted the book into her arms and sauntered over to the wooden door of the girls' locker room. She pushed it open with her butt and held it for Tinsley to scoot through. The locker room was filled with steam from the showers and smelled like peach lotion and hair gel. "Be prepared, and all that."

"I thought that was the Boy Scout motto," Tinsley teased, throwing her coat into one of the metal lockers.

"Whatever. I spent a lot time with them, too." Isla quickly tugged her dress up over her shoulders and dropped it onto the wooden bench in the middle of the alcove.

"Thank God I shaved my legs this morning," Tinsley said, unzipping her gray Rich & Skinny jeans.

"You sure you're ready for this?" Isla asked, waving her own bright yellow bikini from her finger. She scanned Tinsley critically, as if measuring her capacity for illicit behavior.

"If you knew me, you wouldn't even ask."

Five minutes later, Tinsley and Isla raced outside, into the bright January afternoon. It was a sunny day, and the glare off the brilliant white snow was almost blinding. Immediately Tinsley felt goose bumps break out over every bit of visible flesh—which was most of it. The tiny red Shoshanna bikini barely covered her breasts, and the bottom was even skimpier. Tinsley felt like she should be on a beach in Brazil instead of the snowy tundra of upstate New York. Isla confidently strode out into the middle of the quad, her yellow bathing suit bright against the white snow background. She still wore her tall black riding boots.

Tinsley, with her heavy lace-up Uggs, followed her out into the yard. Never before had she felt so aware of her own body. Every inch of it felt electrified. Freezing, but electrified. A group of girls in track pants and sweatshirts descending the steps of the dance studio next to the gym started giggling and pointing.

"Isn't this awesome?" Isla demanded, throwing her arms around a snowman that stood in the quad in front of the gym. Tinsley squinted. She could see Stansfield Hall in the distance. What if Dean Dresden looked out his second-floor office window right now and saw his daughter frolicking around in the snow, sans clothing?

"Cold, but awesome."

"Blow him a kiss!" Tinsley directed, holding up her expensive digital SLR. Isla danced around the snowman like a nymph, slinging her arm around it. The late-afternoon sun was setting behind the classroom buildings, and long shadows were creeping across the quad. But Isla was still in the sunlight, and her dark hair and smooth skin looked striking against the white snow that glittered like diamonds.

Tinsley was amazed. Isla had a perfect body—a little curvier than Tinsley's own, which just made Isla look a little more grown-up. And the way she moved, she looked . . . completely uninhibited. Like she always walked around her new boarding school wearing a bikini and playing in the snow.

Tinsley clicked away, feeling a crowd start to stop and gather around them. Conversations got louder, and were coupled by male hoots of excitement. In their heavy coats with their thick scarves wound around their necks, everybody else seemed so *repressed*.

"Your turn!" Isla grabbed the camera, and Tinsley did a pirouette in the snow. For some reason, she felt like one of the wild fairies in *A Midsummer Night's Dream*, even though it was January, in the middle of the day. Laughing, she made a snowball and started a mock snowball fight with the snowman, then pressed her cheek to his and grabbed his stick-arm as if they were slow dancing.

She might be freezing, but at least she wasn't boring.

OwlNet

JulianMcCafferty: Missed U at dinner tonite.

TinsleyCarmichael: Sorry, kinda busy working on this project w/ Isla. Let's have breakfast mañana?

JulianMcCafferty: You're working w/ Isla? I thought we were going to work together?

TinsleyCarmichael: What? No, I didn't think we decided on anything. Did we?

JulianMcCafferty: I guess not.

TinsleyCarmichael: Good, cuz we already started. You'll be good w/o me, right?

JulianMcCafferty: Yeah, okay. Have fun with Isla.

TinsleyCarmichael: I definitely will. Smooches.

AlanStGirard: Holy shit. Did U hear Tinsley and the dean's hot
daughter had an almost-naked photo shoot out
on the quad?

[No response from HeathFerro.]

AlanStGirard: Tinsley. Dean's daughter. Bikinis. Quad. Tell me
you were there and got pics?

TeagueWilliams: I was there, man, but too stunned to take a
pic.

AlanStGirard: You're useless. Where's Ferro when you need
him? He'd have gotten a pic!

TeagueWilliams: Dude, Ferro's living in the woods, eating
squirrel and shit.

AlanStGirard: WTF???

TeagueWilliams: Jan Plan, man. Crazy times.

WildernessMan Log: Heath vs. Wild

Day 2

Woke before dawn to the sounds of screeching birds. Who knew birds were so damn loud?

Noon temp: 23 degrees F. Thought it was supposed to be warmer. I guess if Bear Grylls can survive in Siberia, HF can make it here!

Food: Spent three hours fashioning a twine net to catch birds. Hung it between two trees. Spent four hours watching birds fly over it. Finally caught rabbit in snare trap. Furry and cute. Felt bad eating it but starving. Searched for berries but the fucking birds ate them all first. Guess I have to get up earlier tomorrow.

Warmth: Starting to feel effects of cold. The challenge is on.

Mood: Good. Tired. Will sleep well. Heard some cross-country skiers laughing in the distance. Either that or hyenas. Wonder if there's a party tonight. Could use a beer after all my hard work, but a good night's sleep will have to do.

A POLITE OWL KNOWS WHEN TO SAY THANK YOU.

Jenny strode across the Waverly quad Wednesday morning, ArtBin in hand. She was eager to get started on her art project and had woken, showered, and dressed before nine. The quad was nearly empty—Waverly students took their sleeping in seriously.

Kara Whalen, wearing dark leggings tucked into her Uggs, nearly knocked Jenny over as she rushed down the path. "Sorry, Jenny. I'm late for my French immersion class. We're going to Paris at the end of it!"

"*Bonne chance,*" Jenny cried, watching Kara disappear into the language building. She shook the snow off her boots and stepped carefully across the freshly polished wood floor of Maxwell Hall, the student center. She always felt terrible for the poor janitors who worked so hard to make the floors sparkle only to be covered again, minutes later, by slush tracked in by dozens of Waverly feet.

The whir of coffee machines filled Jenny's ears as she entered the enormous stone-arched common room. Maxwell was one of her favorite buildings on campus. It was the original chapel, but it had been turned into the student center, and it made Jenny feel like she'd stepped into an old castle. It always smelled like coffee and cinnamon raisin bagels. The art deco–tiled café tables spread across the room were half filled with other early risers huddled over cups of coffee. Jenny quickly paid for a cappuccino and looked around for a seat.

Celine Colista, a senior co-captain of the field hockey team, waved at Jenny. She was parked at a café table with Lon Baruzza, the scholarship kid who worked in the dining hall and had a reputation for being a player. Books and notebooks were spread out in front of them. Celine sported the clean-faced, ponytailed, sweatpants look popular among lazy Waverly Owls after long nights.

"You guys look like you're working hard." Jenny paused at their table as she picked up three packets of Splenda. "Isn't Jan Plan supposed to be a chance to recharge?"

"I've always wanted to read *Anna Karenina*," Celine gushed, holding up a library copy of the fat book. "But I had no idea Lon did, too . . . until we were talking about it at the First Night party. So he was sweet enough to join me. We're going to write a paper about the *tragic* female heroine." She pressed the back of her hand to her forehead theatrically.

Jenny glanced at Lon, who gave her a sly grin. From the way he'd been staring at the pretty, olive-skinned Celine, it was clear that Lon was much more interested in *her* than in Tolstoy. "That sounds like fun, I guess."

Jenny set herself up in an overstuffed armchair by the fire-place, which gave her a good view of the door as people started to stream through, eager to wake up with a cup of coffee and a bagel. She quickly set her supplies out, feeling the rush of excitement she always had when starting a new project. She cracked open her new set of Derwent graphite pencils, all neatly sharpened. With a deep breath, she started to sketch. First she set to work on the stationary objects, which would be completely sharp in her drawing. She sketched the ornate, arched doorway, the garbage can with the flip top, the bottles in the overflowing recycling bin, the empty mugs collecting along the counter. When she had set the scene, she began to sketch the people themselves. Or, rather, their bodies as they moved through space. A couple of guys tossing an orange back and forth came through the door, and Jenny hurriedly tried to capture the arc of the fruit as it sailed through the air.

"Looking good."

Jenny almost jumped out of her skin. Leaning against the back of her chair was Isaac Dresden, wearing a navy blue pea-coat and a pair of dark jeans. He pulled off his red wool hat, his short, dark curls standing up with static. Jenny's heart beat faster. "Excuse me?"

Isaac pointed a half-eaten biscotti toward her sketchbook. It sat in her lap, open to her half-finished drawing of the orange traveling through the air. "Your drawing." Jenny noticed a tiny patch of blond hair, in the middle of his dark waves, right above his left ear. It reminded Jenny of her cat, Marx, who was all black except for a patch of white on his belly.

"Oh, thanks." Jenny blushed, embarrassed to be comparing Isaac to her cat. "Actually, I guess I should be thanking you."

"Me? What for?" Isaac moved off the back of Jenny's chair and sat down on the coffee table in front of her. He slid his black canvas backpack onto the floor.

"I get to pretty much draw all day, because of you." Jenny suddenly felt shy. She closed her sketchbook and took a sip of her coffee, praying that she wouldn't dribble any down the front of her slightly snug navy blue J. Crew V-neck. It had an embroidered *J* above her heart and was an ironic Christmas present from her brother, Dan. He'd told her it would help her remember who she was at chichi boarding school. Now, however, she was worried that it was drawing unneeded attention to her already ample chest. "It was really nice of you to take up my case in your dad's office."

Isaac shrugged. She was acutely aware of how close his knees were to her own. "Well, I have some experience in that area. I kind of know what he needs to hear."

"I appreciate it." Jenny's tongue felt heavy in her mouth, but she was determined not to feel nervous. Isaac was just another boy, after all. A very cute one, and the dean's son, of course. But still just a boy. "It must be kind of weird to go to school where your dad's, you know, in charge."

Isaac took a sip from his stainless steel coffee mug. He still hadn't taken off his coat, which Jenny disappointedly took as a sign that he wasn't staying. "We're used to it by now, me and Isla. He was headmaster at St. Albans, in Connecticut, for a couple years. And he taught at Milton, back when we were younger."

"Why'd you guys come here?" Jenny asked, curiously.

"The official answer is that it was a step up for my dad." Isaac lowered his voice and tilted his chin down mysteriously.

"And the unofficial answer?"

He grinned flirtatiously. "I don't know if you've earned that yet."

"And what does one have to do to earn it?" Her eyes widened. She couldn't believe she was being so bold.

"I don't know." Isaac rubbed his chin. "Go on a walk with me later."

Jenny blushed, flattered. She liked Isaac. And, of course, everyone was talking about how hot he was. It seemed incredible that of everyone at Waverly, he was interested in *her*. But she still didn't feel totally comfortable about the fact that he'd practically gotten her Jan Plan project approved for her. Had she received special treatment? And was she okay with that? "That's really nice of you. But, uh . . . I think I'll probably be working all day," Jenny stammered. Her pencil fell from her hand, and she quickly leaned down to pick it up.

Isaac stood up. "That's cool." He looked a little disappointed, but not put out. He slung his backpack on his shoulder. "Maybe a rain check, then." He tapped her drawing with his finger. "Good luck."

As Isaac walked away, Jenny couldn't keep her eyes from following him. Ten minutes ago, she'd been in one of those creative bubbles where all she could think about was her drawing.

But suddenly, the idea of working on her project all day long, alone, no longer seemed quite so exciting.

OwlNet   Instant Message Inbox

CelineColista: Just saw hot dean's son practically drooling all over Jenny in Maxwell.

VerenaArneval: How does she get all the good ones?

CelineColista: Must be the boobs! =) Totally unfair.

VerenaArneval: Don't complain. I heard Lon bought you a soy latte today. It must be love.

CelineColista: Eh. Lon could do in a pinch. But I'd rather get in good with the dean!

11

A WAVERLY OWL KNOWS WHAT SHE WANTS.

Callie crossed her arms and tapped the pointy toe of her Tory Burch ankle boot against the marble floor of the Reynolds Atrium. The two-story glass-ceilinged space was designed by a world-famous architect and funded by Ryan Reynolds's billionaire father. Normally, Callie avoided the atrium when possible—it always made her feel like she owed Ryan something, and he was the last guy a girl wanted to be indebted to. But the lobby area, filled with potted trees and comfy couches, was perfect for a large group of people to casually get together. Callie had set out a tray of Oreos and Chips Ahoy! cookies on the heavy antique coffee table in the center of one of the conversation nooks. It was almost two on Wednesday afternoon, and her stupid partner was nowhere in sight.

What could Brandon be doing that was so important? Reluctantly, she pulled a tripod from the heavy canvas bag of equipment she'd borrowed from the audiovisual department and started to fumble with its legs. She'd decided to record the interviews so that she could focus on her questions and not get distracted trying to write everything down.

"You're late," she snapped at Brandon when he finally breezed through the revolving glass door five minutes later, stuffing his BlackBerry into his pocket. She stood up, pushing an escaped blond lock out of her face with the back of her hand.

"Sorry." He pulled off his olive green cashmere hat and dusted the snow off the shoulders of his black Diesel bomber jacket. He casually tossed both hat and jacket over the back of an armchair covered with lemon yellow canvas. "I was talking to Hellie."

"I just wish you'd take this a little more seriously." Callie frowned slightly as she planted the borrowed video camera on top of the tripod, pointing it toward the Oreos. She was seriously hopeless with any sort of electronics—it was a defect inherited from her technophobic mother.

Brandon blinked. His eyes were slightly red, as if he wasn't sleeping right, and his chin was still kind of scruffy. Had he left all his razors in Switzerland? "Okay, I'll try to be serious." He coughed into his fist, trying to cover the smirk on his face. "What's the camera for, anyway?"

"I thought it would be easier than taking notes. We can go over everyone's responses later." Callie glared at him. He wasn't even offering to help. Old Brandon Buchanan would have been falling all over himself so that she wouldn't have to raise her pinky finger.

"Nice thinking." Brandon's phone beeped, and he pulled it out of his pocket to read the text.

Callie rolled her eyes and stood up, smoothing the sides of her silky plaid Theory miniskirt. At least she looked more like herself today, wearing a crisp white Ralph Lauren button-down that set off her newly tanned skin. She'd pulled her hair back into a loose bun, with a few blond wisps slipping down into her face. She glanced at the clock on the wall. "I just hope people come."

Brandon pointed toward the wall of windows at the front of the atrium, and Callie turned around just as a group of girls pushed through the revolving doors, clad in thick scarves and boots. "Not bad," he said, impressed. "Did you tell them you were giving away Prada bags?"

Callie smirked at him, but was secretly pleased. "Can you just make sure the camera's set up to get the whole lounge area?"

She'd e-mailed the old Women of Waverly list last night— virtually all the girls at Waverly were on it, and she was pretty sure they'd want to gossip about their love lives. Apparently, she'd been right. Jenny, Tinsley, and all their friends had shown up. "Welcome, ladies," Callie announced brightly. "Just grab a seat wherever." She waved the girls toward the couches as Brandon leaned over the camera, adjusting the lens. Callie was momentarily distracted by the sight. Brandon *did* have a completely cute posterior, especially in his faded Earl jeans.

He glanced back at her. "Cal? Are we ready?"

Callie shook her head clear. "You just operate the camera. I'll ask the questions." The girls had all scattered around on the comfy coral-colored Pottery Barn couches in the lounge area and were looking up at her for instruction. Most of them were dressed in their relaxed, bumming-around clothes: track pants, sweatshirts, Uggs. During the regular semester, most Waverly girls wouldn't be caught dead looking so frumpy, but somehow, Jan Plan was a different animal. "Thank you, ladies, for coming. Help yourselves to the cocoa and cookies over there." She took a deep breath. "Basically, I'm just going to ask some questions. I want to hear from everyone, so really, don't be shy."

"You didn't tell us there were going to be *guys* here," Celine hissed, leaning forward from one of the couches in her gray Waverly track pants and fleece sweatshirt. "I just came from Pilates. I look like shit." Callie glanced over her shoulder at Brandon, who was pretending not to listen.

"It's okay, sweetie." Benny Cunningham, who wore her pearl pendant even to field hockey practice, nudged Celine in the ribs. "True love doesn't care about sweat."

"So, does that mean you guys believe in true love?" Callie broke in, eager to get the meeting on track. She slunk into an armchair and crossed her legs at the knee. She imagined herself leading a talk show and used her best Tyra Banks voice.

A chorus of girls answered immediately in the affirmative. "Um, of course!" Verena Arneval pushed her short, pixieish hair off her forehead. "It might not all be like *The Princess Bride*, but it's got to be out there, right?"

"Do you believe in love at first sight?" Callie asked, chewing on her pen. She was trying really hard not to think of Easy. She'd known him before they'd starting dating, of course, since Waverly was small. And she'd thought he was cute and sexy and arty, but it wasn't love at first sight or anything. More like an instant chemical reaction, the moment he touched her. After that, they couldn't keep their hands off each other, but things were never merely physical. It was like they had this deep, almost mystical connection—and despite their completely obvious differences, they both felt it.

"Definitely," Jenny spoke up. She hadn't meant to be the first person to answer, but she'd been thinking about Isaac, the way their eyes had met across the crowded chapel. Maybe it wasn't necessarily *love*—not yet, at least—but it was something. "Doesn't everyone?" she asked, leaning against a fat pillow in the corner of the couch.

"No way," Kara Whalen interjected. Callie eyed her carefully. Kara had an interesting romantic résumé: after having a brief girl-fling with Brett, she'd started dating Heath Ferro, the self-proclaimed biggest player at Waverly. "Or, at least, it's overrated. Maybe there's a connection—but don't you have to know someone before you fall in love?"

"I don't know." Benny bit her pearly pink lips. "I think it's totally possible to know someone for years, and then one day . . . you just sort of see them in a different light." She glanced, not so subtly, toward the camera, fluffing up her hair.

"That's so boring," Celine announced, snatching an Oreo from the platter Callie had set on the coffee table. She took a tiny nibble, then looked up at the camera. As if suddenly remembering that the chocolate cookie might glom on to her teeth, she set it down on the table. "Of course there's love at first sight—maybe it's just not literally, you know, the *first* sight. But yeah—haven't we all had that moment where you look up and meet some guy's eye, and there's just this amazing jolt of connection?"

"But isn't that just lust?" Rifat Jones, the gangly captain of the girls' volleyball team, shifted in her chair, pulling her sweat-dampened hair into a ponytail. Her Adidas gym bag sat at her feet. "How can you fall in love with someone you don't know?"

Verena batted her eyelashes at the camera. "That's the best way to do it," she said, running her bloodred fingernails through her curls. The other girls giggled and adjusted their hair, almost collectively. Callie bit the inside of her cheek. It was weird that all these girls who showed up practically in their pajamas would be so concerned with how they looked on camera. Didn't they realize that only Callie would be reviewing the footage? Maybe they thought it would be a part of her presentation, when all the Jan Plan projects were presented at the end of the month.

"Do you think it can only happen once? That people only have *one* true love?" Callie's heart pounded as she asked the question. Though she didn't want to admit it, this was what she most wanted to know—and kind of why she'd come up with this project in the first place. Was there hope for her after Easy? Or did she just happen to peak early in the love department? Was she destined to spend the rest of her life alone?

"No," Sage Francis announced, sounding kind of cranky. She glanced back at the camera, too, giving it a funny look. "But the first one is always the hardest to forget, right?"

Callie glanced over her shoulder. Brandon was leaning against the end table, looking bored, his T-shirt gaping away from his stomach and revealing a sliver of squash-toned abs. It was then that Callie realized: the girls weren't interested in the camera, they were interested in *Brandon*. Sage, who'd dated Brandon a few months ago before abruptly dumping him, seemed particularly interested in getting his attention. It was so weird. Brandon stopped shaving and got a girlfriend, and suddenly all the girls were sneaking glances and sticking their chests out at him.

Now that Callie had figured out what was going on, it seemed ridiculously obvious. She stuck to her list of questions, but as they began to get more personal, the girls took longer to answer, glancing up at Brandon for cues. Callie felt like a scientist who realized her experiment had been contaminated. These girls were clearly not being honest—they were just trying to look good in front of a guy. And Brandon, no less.

After a chorus of girls agreed that true love was something that almost always happened to a girl in high school, Callie took a deep breath. Her irritation grew when Benny announced that she could only fall in love with a musician—Brandon, of course, played the violin in the Waverly orchestra. Even more annoying was when, apropos of nothing, Celine said she always found herself attracted to guys with golden brown eyes, a feature, not coincidentally, that Brandon shared.

That was it. Not only were these lying harpies totally ruining her experiment, but if Brandon was going to be interested in anyone in this room, it would obviously be Callie. He'd been in love with her practically forever, and even if he wasn't at *this exact moment*, it was only because he was distracted by his Swiss mountain girl. He'd called his relationship with Callie "ancient history," but it wasn't *so* long ago, was it?

Before she knew what she was doing, she got to her feet and waltzed toward him. He was standing behind the camera, arms crossed over his chest.

He looked up in surprise as Callie leaned toward him. "What's up?" he asked under his breath. He wore a navy blue Ralph Lauren crewneck over a plain white T-shirt, looking sexier than ever. Was this Sebastian all over again? Was Callie only attracted to Brandon now because all the other girls were, too?

Only one way to find out.

The room grew noticeably quieter as the girls struggled to overhear Callie and Brandon's conversation. Defiantly, she placed her hand on Brandon's back and put her mouth close to his ear. She almost fainted at the familiar smell of his Acqua di Parma cologne.

"How's the camera working?" she drawled, making sure to let her Georgia accent sweeten her words. Brandon always used to say it made him weak in the knees.

"The camera?" Brandon straightened up, a confused look on his handsome face. He shrugged his shoulders. "I think it's fine."

"Excellent." Callie tossed her hair over her shoulder and leaned down to look through the camera. She saw the eyes of the girls focused firmly on her. Celine's arms were crossed over her chest, and she had that pinched, irritated look on her face she always got whenever someone stepped between her and a guy.

Callie stared right back, a smug smile twitching at the corners of her lips. Suddenly, nothing seemed more important than showing these girls that Brandon was *her* partner. And Callie wasn't positive, but she thought she'd caught a glimpse of something familiar in Brandon's eyes—something that said maybe he wasn't totally immune to her charms.

Maybe ancient history wasn't so ancient, after all.

From: BrettMesserschmidt@waverly.edu
To: CallieVernon@waverly.edu
Date: Wednesday, January 5, 3:34 P.M.
Subject: Re: The Science of Love

Hey Cal,

Sorry I couldn't make it to your interview session today—I got caught up in my project with Chrissy. But I'd still love to help—let me know if you need someone else to interview later.

BTW, you're going to love this—like four girls have asked me if there's anything going on between you and Brandon. And they all seemed pretty jealous. HA!

Xo

B

OwlNet   Instant Message Inbox

JennyHumphrey: Still interested in taking that walk? Maybe after dinner?

IsaacDresden: You cashing in that rain check already?

JennyHumphrey: It seems like such a shame to work all day. . . .

IsaacDresden: Exactly. Why don't you meet me at the field house at 7? Dress warmly, okay?

JennyHumphrey: Uh-oh. What do U have in mind?

IsaacDresden: Just a walk in the winter wonderland.

12

A WAVERLY OWL SHOULD NOT OBSESS OVER THE PAST—OR PAST GIRLFRIENDS.

"What do you think about this?" Chrissy asked, wrapping a swatch of yellow floral fabric around a naked Barbie doll's waist. "For Fantine?"

Brett tilted her head so that her red hair swung down to her shoulders. "I think whoever plays Fantine better not be shy."

The two girls were holed up in a sunny upstairs alcove of Maxwell Hall on Wednesday night, their magazine clippings and swatches of fabric spread out across the slightly sticky coffee table. That morning, they'd climbed into Chrissy's rickety orange Volkswagen Rabbit and spent hours at the fabric store in downtown Rhinecliff, rummaging through bins of sale scraps. "And that fabric looks like it belongs to Laura Ingalls."

"What, you don't think we should go in the Little Stripper on the Prairie direction?" Chrissy asked innocently, twisting Barbie back and forth.

"I think it's weird that you keep a stash of Barbie dolls under your bed, by the way." Brett leaned back in her chair and took a sip of her steaming latte. She tugged at the neck of her slim-fitting chocolate brown Joie turtleneck. "Don't tell Heath Ferro—it's probably some fantasy of his."

"They're only naked until I can design clothes for them," Chrissy insisted, adjusting Barbie's arms and legs so that she posed in a very risqué handstand. "And besides—I bet Heath Ferro's the kind of guy who has plenty of dolls of his own stashed under his bed."

Brett almost snorted foam up her nose as she and Chrissy dissolved into giggles. She hadn't expected the project to be so fun. Last Jan Plan, she'd spent the month translating a bunch of Greek poetry with Celine Colista. Brett had never thought of herself as an artistic person before—she certainly wasn't as creative as Jenny, who was always making amazing sketches of random things she'd seen, like a tipped-over garbage can or an apple core. But Chrissy, whose taste was a weird combination of classic and bizarre, made Brett feel like she was an essential part of this team. She was the straight foil to Chrissy's out-there sensibilities.

"You know what would look great for the soldiers—what about Nehru jackets?" Brett scooted to the edge of the couch and leaned forward over the coffee table. She flipped through one of their photography books until she found a picture of the Beatles, in their trip-to-India-to-find-Buddha-and-get-high days, wearing long, colorful jackets with banded collars.

"You're brilliant!" Chrissy squealed, pushing her bleached-blond hair behind her ears. "I think that's awesome." She leaned back and stared dreamily up at the slanted dark wood ceiling beams, as if she were already picturing it.

"Mr. Shepard's okay with this being unconventional, right?"

"You think this is unconventional?" She tapped her forehead. "Once, when Seb and I were together, he took me to this off-off Broadway performance of *Cats* where all the actors were dressed up as dogs." Chrissy laughed, as if reliving the experience. "They were still meowing and shit—it was bizarre."

Brett's heart almost stopped beating. She felt her body slide back down into the leather couch. "When you and Sebastian were together?" she repeated.

Seeing the look on Brett's face, Chrissy dropped the Barbie doll she'd been holding. It clunked loudly against the worn hardwood floor. "Oh, you're kidding. I thought you knew." Her wide blue eyes widened with concern. "He didn't tell you?"

"No, he didn't." Suddenly Brett's stomach dropped. Why wouldn't Sebastian have told her about Chrissy? He knew about Jeremiah, after all. Brett had talked about the whole sordid saga of their relationship—in fact, she'd told Sebastian even before they'd starting dating, when he was still just her tutee. But why had they never had a conversation about *his* exes?

"Well, probably because it wasn't a big deal. It was only, like, a few months." Chrissy shrugged apologetically. She looked really worried, and it touched Brett that she was so concerned about her feelings.

But a *few months* in high school was like . . . five *years* in the real world. *Everyone* knew that. Brett and Jeremiah had really only been together for a few months, yet she'd been completely in love with him. And had almost slept with him.

"I'm just kind of surprised he didn't tell you," Chrissy said softly.

Brett leaned over and picked up the naked Barbie doll from the floor, just to have something to do with her hands. So the postcard on Chrissy's wall hadn't been totally platonic. She wondered what Sebastian had written on the back of it. Her throat tightened when she remembered what he'd said to her as he gave her the framed photograph of the Italian village. That he wanted to take her there someday. Had he said the same thing to Chrissy?

Brett sucked in her cheeks and forced a smile to her lips. "Yeah, me too."

 **OwlNet**   Instant Message Inbox

BrettMesserschmidt: Can I ask U something? Discreetly?

BennyCunningham: Sounds juicy! Ask away.

BrettMesserschmidt: Do U know who Sebastian dated? Before me?

BennyCunningham: Besides Chrissy?

BrettMesserschmidt: Got that one. Anyone else?

BennyCunningham: Hmmm. Saw him getting all cozy w/ Alexis O'Donnell at an open mic night.

BrettMesserschmidt: That chick who's always lugging around her acoustic guitar and singing "Kumbaya"? Seriously?

BennyCunningham: Looked pretty serious. U should ask Devon Sprague. U know she keeps a little black book of all Waverly hookups to sell on eBay someday when we're all rich and famous!

BrettMesserschmidt: Perfect.

13

A WAVERLY OWL MUST OBTAIN PERMISSION TO
LEAVE CAMPUS AFTER CURFEW.

It was dark by the time Jenny stepped onto the unshov-
eled sidewalk that led to the Field House. She shivered in
the cold night, rubbing the arms of her red Gap peacoat.
Her small hands were covered by the cute white Anthropol-
ogie gloves Brett had given her for Christmas, but the thin
angora wasn't made for snowy days in upstate New York, and
her fingers felt like icicles. At least her legs were warm under
her Citizens jeans—she had on a pair of thick wool stockings.
Totally worth it, even if they made her look a little thicker than
normal. A cold breeze picked up, chilling Jenny's face, and she
wondered why she'd been so urgent to have her walk with Isaac
tonight. It could have waited until tomorrow.

But then she caught sight of him, sitting on the steps outside the Field House, a gray canvas messenger bag slung across
the shoulder of his navy coat. A thick cream-colored wool scarf

was tucked casually around his neck. He looked totally adorable, in a British-prep-school way. He straightened up when he saw her, the electric grin lighting up his face. Her stomach flipped.

That was why she came.

"I like your hat."

Jenny touched her head automatically. She was wearing her ancient navy-and-white cap with the snowflake pattern. It once had a pom-pom on top, which had since, thankfully, disappeared. "Thanks. A present from my grandma, about a million years ago."

Isaac stood up and dusted off his pants. "It's still pretty cute."

Jenny felt her cheeks flush, which helped fight the cold. Not that she was thinking about the cold anymore. "So, where do you want to go? I'll be your tour guide."

"What's this place called the crater that I keep hearing about?" Isaac asked, stuffing his gloved hands in his pockets. He raised his eyebrows mysteriously. "I heard something about animal sacrifices, and naturally I was intrigued."

"The crater?" Jenny repeated. The crater was, of course, a notorious place on campus for partying. It was just beyond the edge of campus, a big granite crater in the woods that felt like a kind of sunken living room when filled with Waverly students. Heath Ferro had thrown his big End-of-the-World party there a few months ago, when the trees were covered with golden autumn leaves. It would be kind of interesting to see it covered in snow. But it was late already, and it was a bad idea to be caught that far off campus, even during laid-back Jan Plan. Technically, students weren't allowed to leave campus in the evenings without a special pass. Jenny was pretty sure that wanting to take a romantic moonlit walk with her new crush would not have qualified her for one. "Well, that's kind of off-limits."

"I was joking about the animal sacrifices, by the way." A look of worry crossed Isaac's face. "Did it come out weird?"

Jenny giggled. She breathed onto her frozen hands, hoping to bring feeling back to them. "It's not that. I just don't want to get in trouble."

"I'm sure it'll be fine, right?" Isaac glanced around. "It's not like we're hauling a keg out there or anything. Although I did bring refreshments." He pulled a stainless steel thermos from his bag. "Hot chocolate."

"Nonalcoholic, I hope." Jenny giggled, watching her breath turn into vapor in the dark night air. Isaac somehow managed to make her feel nervous and comfortable at once. It was so sweet of him to bring hot chocolate. It made her think of the horse-drawn carriages that clomped through Central Park with happy couples snuggled under wool blankets.

Isaac snapped his fingers in mock disappointment, but in his thick gloves, his fingers didn't exactly snap. "I didn't even *think* of spiking it. I guess I'm still learning." They headed toward the woods, away from the warm yellow lights shining through the windows of dorm rooms. In the distance, Jenny could hear a few students heading to Maxwell for the open mic night that a group of seniors had organized, and the faint strumming of a guitar. Even though their laughing voices sounded happy, Jenny was right where she wanted to be.

"So . . ." Jenny asked, curling her toes in her boots to keep them warm. Up ahead, the woods loomed, and she thought of the Robert Frost poem with the line "The woods are lovely, dark, and deep." "You like Waverly so far?"

Isaac glanced sideways at her. "It's got its pluses." Then he laughed. "I signed up to take a class instead of doing an independent project. I'm taking beginning Mandarin."

"Wow." Jenny rubbed her hands together. Waverly offered intensive courses in each of the foreign languages it taught over Jan Plan for students who wanted to get ahead. "That sounds ambitious."

Isaac grinned. "I don't know. I kind of like a challenge." He raised his eyebrows suggestively and held a snow-covered pine tree bough out of the way as Jenny stepped onto the path to the crater. "I mean, academically."

"Of course." Jenny giggled and ducked under the branch. "I hope I can still find the way. The last time I was here, it wasn't exactly snow-covered." But just as she said that, the narrow path opened into a clearing. A giant saucer-shaped depression lay in front of them, covered in a foot of perfect, untrammeled snow. "Ah! Ta-da!"

"Perfect." Isaac headed toward one of the giant logs at the edge of the crater. Enterprising Owls had dragged fallen trees around the edges of the depression years ago, to create a kind of sunken amphitheater. He swiped his gloves across it, sending the snow flurrying to the ground. Then he pulled a thick fleece blanket from his bag and spread it out across the top of the log. "And now you don't have to freeze your butt off."

"I've never had such service before." Jenny pressed the back of her hand to her forehead in a fake swoon, sitting down on the blanket. Isaac twisted the cap off the thermos and poured a steaming cup of hot chocolate for Jenny. "But I guess I've also never been on a winter picnic before."

"You're missing out." The aroma of cocoa combined with the healthy pine smell of the forest and Jenny settled in, wrapping the corner of the blanket over her lap. Isaac sat down next to her, the sleeve of his thick coat brushing slightly against her own. There were so many layers between them, but Jenny still felt a little charge.

She took a tiny sip of the steaming liquid. "This is delicious."

Isaac grinned. "It's an old recipe . . . also known as Swiss Miss." He fumbled through his bag for something else and pulled out a pair of dark gloves. "I forgot—I brought extra gloves, in case you needed them." Before she knew what he was doing, he had grabbed her hand and was holding it in his. "Yours don't really seem warm enough."

Her gloves weren't, but her hand still felt the electricity of his touch jolt through them. Reluctantly, she pulled her hand away, taking the extra pair of gloves with her. "You're so prepared," she teased, but really she was incredibly flattered. How was it even possible that Isaac could be so thoughtful? He was a teenage boy, after all.

Isaac rubbed his own hands together and laughed. "I know that you girls are kind of, you know, delicate flowers."

"Hey." Jenny slapped him playfully with her newly warm hand. "I'm no delicate flower. You should have seen me play field hockey this fall."

"You have no idea how sorry I am that I missed it." Isaac laughed. He picked up a tree branch from the ground and raked it across the smooth white snow at the edge of the crater. "You know, you don't seem like all the other prep-school girls."

"What do you mean?" Jenny asked slowly. Not that she minded someone telling her she wasn't like the other Waverly girls. She didn't really *feel* like them—and she'd made her peace with that. But she wanted to know what it was about her that made it so obvious. It couldn't be just that she wore clothing from the Gap.

Isaac shrugged, digging a little hole with the end of the branch. "I dunno. Just 'cause of my dad, we've been around schools like Waverly my whole life. And there's always some cool people . . . but there's always a lot of . . . you know." He stared up at the sky. "Girls who only care about pearl earrings and designer clothes."

"There's plenty of shallow boys here, too," Jenny pointed out. Even as she said it, she kept staring at his gorgeous, full lips and thinking how nice they'd feel to kiss. His mouth was probably warm and cocoa-flavored. "But there's also a lot of nice people."

Isaac looked at Jenny's face thoughtfully. She'd never seen eyes the color of his, an almost celery shade of green. "I like that you watch people. I saw you doing it that first day in the chapel. Your eyes were just sort of taking everything in. Thinking about it." He brushed a lock of dark hair off his forehead. "I kinda thought you might be an artist, then."

Jenny felt her skin start to glow. His eyes were staring right at her in a look that made her feel completely naked. Her lips parted, but she couldn't think what to say.

Just then, a bright light shone on her face. Standing ten feet away from them was Ben, the cranky, middle-aged grounds-keeper, holding his flashlight firmly on their faces. *Gotcha!* his face seemed to scream. He lived for getting kids into trouble.

Jenny squealed and scrambled to her feet, sending her cup of hot chocolate spraying across the snow. Ben had famously caught Heath Ferro smoking pot out on the soccer fields last year, and Heath had to bribe him with his expensive Cartier watch in order to keep his mouth shut. The groundskeeper probably had no need for Jenny's pink Swatch watch.

But Isaac got to his feet calmly. "Oh, hey, Mr. Greenwood." He stepped toward Ben, who had reluctantly lowered his light. "Nice night for a walk, huh?"

To her complete surprise, the old man actually chuckled. "I don't know about that." He shook his head slowly. "Awfully chilly. But you kids keep warm, y'hear?"

Isaac laughed and casually draped his arm over Jenny's shoulder. "Thanks, Mr. Greenwood. You want any hot chocolate?"

Ben laughed again and turned. "No, thanks. I've got some soup on the stove, waiting for me to get home. G'night." Jenny stared after him as he marched away.

It took a minute before she found her voice. "I think that just took three years off my life." She pressed her gloves to her heart as if to slow it down.

"You okay?"

Jenny was acutely aware of the fact that Isaac's arm was still on her shoulder. "It's just . . . I don't think I've ever seen that man crack a smile before."

Isaac laughed and stepped away from Jenny. "Mr. Greenwood? He's a puppy dog."

Jenny settled back onto the log. "A puppy dog? Normally he's a Rottweiler." Her heart was still beating from the surprise of getting caught. "You know, I've actually kind of been in trouble before. I totally felt like it was going to happen again."

"You? In trouble? Now that's a story I want to hear." Isaac leaned over to pick up Jenny's fallen cup. He dusted the snow off with his sleeve and refilled it for her. "Refill?" he said, holding it out.

Jenny smiled and took the cup of cocoa, but she couldn't relax completely. She was grateful that the groundskeeper wasn't going to bust her for being off campus, but she was starting to wonder how this whole dating-the-dean's-son thing was going to work.

But then she caught Isaac smiling at her and decided she might be okay with special treatment, after all.

From: BrettMesserschmidt@waverly.edu
To: DevonSprague@waverly.edu
Date: Wednesday, January 5, 3:43 P.M.
Subject: Coffee?

Devon,

Hope you're taking full advantage of Jan Plan and relaxing and enjoying the snow.

Listen, I was wondering if you'd mind doing a little favor for a field hockey teammate? I was just hoping for a little background info on someone and I heard you were the right person to talk to. Can I buy you a cup of coffee? Today or tomorrow? Let me know!

Brett

From: DevonSprague@waverly.edu
To: BrettMesserschmidt@waverly.edu
Date: Wednesday, January 5, 5:23 P.M.
Subject: Re: Coffee?

Brett,

Mmm, sounds intriguing. How about tomorrow at 11am? If this is about who I think it's about, we'll have a lot to talk about. =)

See you then!

D

WildernessMan Log: Heath vs. Wild

Day 3

Woke up in the middle of the night to what looked like my mother's overweight Persian cat digging through my pack. I called out its name, *Here Peeshie, Here Peeshie* before I realized that it wasn't my mother's cat but a goddamn raccoon. I yelled and he ran away, a pack of dehydrated ice cream in his teeth. Fucker. My last end-of-day treat. Are raccoons edible? Maybe I'll teach that fattie a lesson and fry him up.

Noon temp: 20 degress F. WTF? Abnormally cold this time of year. Gotta roll with it.

Food: Sat in tree watching snare trap, but squirrels and chipmunks avoiding it. Do they talk to each other? Don't they know I'm just trying to survive? Can't they help a brother out? Went for hike to search for berries, but none exist. Even looked for bugs to eat, but none big enough to have any nutritional value. Broke into my emergency jerky reserves. Hate to have to do that so early, but feeling kind of weak. Not sure it's all from hunger.

Warmth: Foot fell asleep this morning for about 45 minutes. Thought it might be frostbite, but eventually feeling returned. Slept w/ BB's sleeping bag wrapped around mine. Helped a little.

Mood: Keep hoping more skiers will come around. Or snowshoers. Gets kind of quiet listening to birds chirp. Kind of lonely, too. But that's what you've gotta deal with when you're a WildernessMan.

A WAVERLY OWL DOES NOT DRINK IN HER DORM ROOM—OR IN THE DEAN'S DAUGHTER'S ROOM.

"Don't even *think* about leaving yet." Isla pressed herself against the closed door of her bedroom on the first floor of the dean's house. The room was very non-Isla—the white four-poster bed was covered with a faded floral quilt trimmed with lace, and frilly white curtains draped across the windows. The walls were painted a shade of cotton-candy pink that only a five-year-old girl who dreamed of being a princess could love. "I've got something that's only fun when shared."

"That sounds intriguing," Tinsley replied, flicking open her phone to check the time. "But I'm supposed to meet Julian soon." They were meeting up in half an hour, and she definitely didn't want to be late. It was Wednesday night, and she'd somehow managed to not see him at all for the past few days. She'd been so busy with Isla, scouting places around campus for photo shoots. They'd just come back from pawing through the overcrowded racks at Next to New, the secondhand clothing store in town, to drop off their bags of loot onto Isla's shaggy white rug.

"Come on." Isla threw her jacket onto her bed and opened the top drawer of her antique-looking bureau. Isla pulled out a bottle of Ketel One from under a pair of black silk pajamas. "We've been working all day. You need to chill out a little first."

Tinsley considered. She could use a pick-me-up—and there was something really illicit and exciting about drinking in the dean's house. Especially when he and his wife were playing backgammon in the living room. "How can I refuse? And nice room, by the way," Tinsley added, giggling.

The room was neat and clean, the only decoration on the pink walls one of the Waverly calendars sent out to parents and alumni. It was filled with scenic campus pictures and "candids" of students looking well fed and healthy in the library and on the quad.

"I think Marymount had a kindergartener with a princess complex." Isla laughed as she grabbed two shot glasses from the drawer. She set the glasses and the bottle on the floor next to a rocking chair. "I kind of dig it. It makes me feel like I'm living in a dollhouse. Besides, it was the only bedroom on the first floor, so I had to take advantage." Isla poured a generous shot of vodka into each of the shot glasses and handed one to Tinsley.

Tinsley sat down on the shaggy white rug and tucked her black tiered Charlotte Ronson skirt around her knees. "Funny, I never saw a dollhouse with a shot glass like this," she laughed, examining her glass. Imprinted on the side was a picture of a hula girl holding up a wreath of flowers over the words *I got lei'd in Maui.*

"I collect them," Isla said proudly, holding up her own glass, which was imprinted with Cyrillic-looking writing. "It says 'Russian girls do it better.'" She shrugged. "I'm half Russian, so I guess I do it half better."

"What are we drinking to?" Tinsley asked, clinking her shot glass against Isla's.

"To new friends." Isla smiled deviously.

Tinsley tossed the liquid down her throat, enjoying the burn. "And to making people stare."

Isla laughed and walked to her closet, pulling off her sweater in a rush of static. She hung it neatly on a hook before throwing on a plain white men's dress shirt, only buttoning half the buttons. Tinsley had always wished she had a brother: not only did it guarantee cute boys around the house, but she also loved wearing men's shirts, and just buying a new white men's button-down from Bloomie's didn't do it for her. You had to have one so worn-in it was tissue-soft with the undeniable scent of a former owner still clinging to it.

Isla flicked on her stereo, and the sounds of The Raconteurs filled the room. She refilled the shot glasses. "Only trouble is, now we have to outdo ourselves."

That afternoon, they'd found a couple of gorgeous vintage prom dresses in the theater department's costume room and had pranced around the crowded dining hall wearing them. Tinsley had worn a delicate, seafoam green satin bodice with a full ballerina-style tulle skirt, while Isla donned a lavender strapless dress with a sweetheart neckline, her hair in a loose upsweep. They took turns photographing each other as they walked through the lunch line, the plastic dining hall trays contrasting with their frilly dresses. All the girls had stared at them jealously, while the guys looked on with dreamy expressions. Tinsley loved the feel of everyone's eyes locked to her, and the sounds of whispers as she strolled by. It felt like the good old days.

Tinsley stretched out her long legs in front of her as she downed another shot. Before she knew it, two hours had passed. Isla was interested in hearing all about Tinsley, and Tinsley loved talking to someone from outside the Waverly bubble.

"Shit," Tinsley exclaimed finally, staring at her phone. The shots of vodka had blurred together and she'd been with Isla for hours longer than she'd planned. It was almost midnight. "I've got to get to Julian's." She jumped to her feet, wavering slightly. She had to put a steadying hand on Isla's dresser as she slid into her black ankle boots.

"Whoa, girl." Isla laughed, swinging her bare feet to the floor. "You sure you can make it out the window?" She hoisted up her window with a noisy squeak.

"Don't worry about me." Tinsley blew her a kiss as she slung her legs through the window and let her body fall gently to the ground. Her head buzzed pleasantly, and the snow glittered in the moonlight. The campus was nearly silent, and all Tinsley could think about was Julian. She was late—really late—and she hoped he hadn't gone to bed yet.

She knocked at his window. Thank God for first-floor bedrooms. The curtains were drawn, but a faint light shone through. She thought she could hear the murmur of music. She knocked harder, her bare knuckles rapping against the cold glass.

Finally, Julian's face appeared at the window. He seemed surprised to see her, but he quickly opened the window and held out a hand. She grabbed it and tried to pull herself up, but the bottoms of her shoes kept sliding down the brick wall. Eventually, she was able to climb over the ledge, her feet landing softly on Julian's floor.

"I must be out of practice." She giggled. She dusted herself off and threw her coat on Julian's roommate's empty bed. "Hey, baby." Tinsley turned to Julian and threw her arms around his neck.

Julian stiffened and gave her a funny smile. "Hey."

"Sorry I'm late." She pressed her cheek to his chest. He felt so warm and delicious. "Isla and I were just having so much fun working on our project. It's just . . . the coolest project ever."

"Uh-huh." Julian disentangled himself from Tinsley's arms and sat down on his bed, yawning. He wore a plain white T-shirt and a pair of striped gray flannel Abercrombie & Fitch pajama bottoms.

"Were you sleeping?" Tinsley teased, crawling into bed with him. "That's so cute."

"I didn't think you were coming." Julian let her kiss him, briefly, before leaning back on his elbows. "And, dude, take your boots off. You're getting snow in my bed."

Tinsley kicked her boots to the floor and then crawled back

next to Julian. "Isla has an amazing eye. We're doing this whole series of photographs of ourselves in these high-contrast poses. Everything looks so gorgeous so far," Tinsley gushed drunkenly.

Julian pushed a piece of pale brown hair out of his face. He smelled like soap, and Tinsley wanted to kiss him all over. "Yeah. I heard what you're doing." He shrugged. "Everyone has."

"What does that mean?" Tinsley sat up straight. She definitely didn't care for his tone. Tiny alarm bells started to go off in her head.

"I don't know. It just seems like . . . an easy project. Two beautiful girls? Taking pictures of each other modeling in skimpy clothes?" Julian shrugged. "Are you sure that's what you really want to be spending your time on? What about directing and film?"

"But it's not like it's just modeling," Tinsley explained, running her finger over Julian's knee. She was starting to get annoyed with him. "It's *art*. Isla has this amazing art book of all these classic photographs of women in these, like, normal settings, but wearing clothes that are completely out of context. It's all about contrast, and the unexpected, and . . ." Tinsley trailed off. The vodka had left her brain sluggish, and she was irritated that her jumbled words didn't do their project justice.

Julian swung his feet to the floor and sat up. "Sorry, but when everyone shares their Jan Plan projects at the end of the month, I don't think the guys at Waverly will be thinking about *contrast* or the *unexpected* when they look at those pictures of you practically naked."

"Julian!" Tinsley got to her feet. "Why are you being such a prude?" Her eyes narrowed. Was that even what this was about? Or was Julian just . . . *jealous*? "Or is this about me choosing to work with Isla instead of you? That's really immature."

"No, it's not that." Julian rolled his eyes. "Look, I'm sorry. You can't blame me for not loving the idea of the entire male population of Waverly ogling my girlfriend in a bikini."

All the blood rushed to Tinsley's face. She'd never felt so insulted before. How could he be so ignorant? Didn't he have any sense of what art was? For the second time in twenty minutes, Tinsley steadied herself on a dresser and slid her feet into her ankle boots. "Then maybe I shouldn't *be* your girlfriend."

She got all the way to the window before realizing that Julian hadn't answered. She glanced back at him. He was still sitting where she'd left him on his bed, his handsome face lit from the side by the moonlight streaming through the window. He stared at her as if he'd never seen her before. It was a mix of disappointment and confusion.

Well, if he wanted to sit there in silence, fine. He could be boring and sit around in his room for the rest of fucking Jan Plan if he wanted, watching movies in his sweatpants all day.

He'd just have to do it without her.

SageFrancis: I was just out snowshoeing with Ryan and I think we saw a bum in the woods.

CelineColista: No, I think that's HEATH. He's doing an outdoor-survival thing, eating berries and building fires.

SageFrancis: Wow, I knew he was dirty, but he looked FILTHY.

CelineColista: If he was horny before, think what a few days without female contact will do.

SageFrancis: Hmmm . . . if only Brandon had some of that wild animal quality, maybe we'd still be together. Tho yesterday he looked . . . different. Good.

CelineColista: Yeah, I saw him, too. The scruffy, jet-lagged look does a body goooood.

SageFrancis: I thought there was something going on with you and Lon?

CelineColista: Hmm, sounds like someone's a little jealous!

A WAVERLY OWL KNOWS THAT SOMEONE IS ALWAYS WATCHING.

Brandon tossed the black rubber squash ball in the air. It was early Thursday afternoon, and he had just finished pulverizing Julian in a very one-sided match. Julian's game had been terrible—normally the tall, gangly freshman was Brandon's biggest challenge on the team. But today he'd been sluggish and distracted, barely making Brandon break a sweat.

"You suck today," Brandon said as they stepped off the clean plastic box of a court. He picked up his Prince sports bag and tucked away his racquet. "My seventy-year-old grandma could have kicked your ass."

"I know." Julian lifted up his T-shirt to wipe the sweat off his forehead. His straw-colored hair was pulled back in a sloppy ponytail, and Brandon was dying to take a pair of scissors and snip it right off. Just because the kid was from Seattle didn't mean he had to look like Kurt Cobain. "Tinsley broke up with me last night."

Brandon dropped his bag. "No shit." He eyed Julian, who had slumped down on the bench. Everyone had been impressed with the way this freshman kid had managed to handle Tinsley Carmichael, one of the hottest—and craziest—girls on campus. But when she was dating Julian, Tinsley actually managed to seem kind of, well, nice. "You all right?"

Julian nodded slowly, but his face had an unhealthy-looking paleness to it. "It just sucks. I don't really know where it came from. Everything was awesome over break, and suddenly we come back here, and it's like she doesn't want to spend any time with me. She practically told me I was too boring."

"Ouch." Brandon sat down on the bench. "That's even worse than being *too nice*, which is what I usually get."

"What's with that?" Julian asked, tossing his racquet back and forth between his hands. "Do they want us to be assholes?"

"I guess." Brandon took a long sip from his water bottle, letting the cold liquid spill over his chin. "Maybe what girls really want is to be ignored. It gives them a challenge. Maybe Tinsley felt like it wasn't as exciting once, you know, the race was over."

"That's fucked up." Julian stared mournfully at the empty squash court.

"Well, girls *are* fucked up, dude." Brandon gave him a manly pat on the back.

Julian forced a smile and snapped his towel at Brandon. "How about another game? I promise I'll kick your ass this time."

Brandon pulled his platinum Cartier watch from his bag and glanced at it. He didn't even have time to shower. "Nah, I've got to run." He was almost due for his daily iChat appointment with Hellie. It was the end of her day in Switzerland, and they liked to talk just before she fell asleep. She said it made for sweet dreams about him. "Some other time. Cheer up, man."

Brandon left his peacoat open as he exited the squash complex, enjoying the feel of the cold, clean air against his sweaty chest. The sun was shining, the sky was a perfect blue, and the snow positively glittered in the light. A pack of Waverly students in cross-country skis raced past him. As he stomped up the steps of Richards to his dorm room, he whistled.

He threw down his squash bag, tossed his coat onto his bed, and immediately opened up his iBook, clicking through the windows to set up for his talk with Hellie. He grinned at the thought of her.

There was a gentle knock at his door. "Come in," Brandon called out, opening his e-mail. He deleted a forward of photos of kittens in Halloween costumes from his grandmother.

Callie took a deep breath when she heard Brandon's voice. Huddled in the hallway, she suddenly had second thoughts. Should she even be here? It felt like ages since she'd been in Brandon's room. In the pocket of her baby blue Searle puffer coat, her gloved hand felt for the pair of earphones Brandon had left at the atrium yesterday. Although she knew it wasn't necessary for her to bring them to his room, she wanted an excuse to see him. Alone. She hadn't been able to stop thinking about him.

Finally, she poked her head into Brandon's room. Her fuzzy cream-colored scarf felt hot around her neck, and she quickly unwound it. "Are you decent?" she called out, jokingly.

And then she caught sight of him leaning over his computer, pushing his sweat-dampened hair off his perfect forehead. His gray T-shirt clung to his well-defined torso.

Why wasn't she this attracted to Brandon when they'd been dating? It would have made everything *so* much better.

"Uh, what's up?" Brandon straightened, shooting Callie a friendly but quizzical look. On the wall above his desk, Callie could see his Waverly calendar thumbtacked to the wall, the tiny squares filled in with notes that read "Mexican night!" and "Call Grams, 7 pm" and "coffee w/ J." Normally, she would have snickered at how dorky it was that Brandon penciled even the tiniest things into his calendar. But now all she could think about was what a great body Brandon had, and how nice it would be to kiss his stomach. And who the hell was J?

Callie blew a strand of hair out of her face and stepped forward. "You, uh, left your earphones at the atrium yesterday. I thought you'd miss them."

"Hey, thanks." Brandon's green eyes lit up. He took the earbuds from Callie's outstretched hand, his fingers brushing against hers lightly. "I've been using my extra pair. But I wondered what happened to those."

Callie felt her knees buckle slightly, and she sat down on Brandon's bed, thinking of all the times they'd made out there. She'd never felt like this—like she *had* to touch him. Suddenly, she felt completely transparent. It was so obvious that she hadn't needed to bring Brandon his earbuds—she could have texted that she had them, or given them to him at lunch.

After a few moments of silence, Callie realized Brandon was waiting for her to say something. "Where's Heath?" She leaned back on her elbows, letting her rose-colored Polo top tighten against her chest, and crossed her legs. Her black wool micromini had crept dangerously high on her thighs. *Look at me*, she tried to tell Brandon telepathically.

Brandon chuckled and leaned against his desk—casually, he hoped. Like he didn't even care that Callie, whom he'd been pining over since the day they broke up, was sitting there, right on his bed. Waiting for him. "You haven't heard? He's living in the fucking woods."

"Oh, right." Callie felt dumb. She knew that. "So, it's like you've got a single for a month."

"Yeah, I guess so." Brandon rubbed his chin. "It's been nice not having to pick his dirty clothes up off the floor."

Callie smiled at the tiny touch of the old Brandon. Since he wasn't coming near her, she stood up and ran her fingers along the edge of his bookshelf. She paused at a silver picture frame with a photo of Brandon and a gorgeous, tall blond girl on a ski slope somewhere. What was her name again? Something horrible, like Heidi or Helga. His *girlfriend*. The blood surged through her veins. In the photo, Brandon had his hand on the girl's lower back. Definitely an intimate touch. Had they really had *sex*? Was *that* what was so different about him? Callie stepped closer to Brandon.

"There are other perks to having a single, you know," she murmured.

"What do you . . ." Brandon started, then gave a funny laugh, as if he finally realized what Callie was talking about. A confused look came into his eyes. "*Callie.* Are you . . . hitting on me?"

Callie's faced flushed as she defiantly tossed her long hair over her shoulder. "I don't know." She hated that she was being so obvious . . . but then she suddenly didn't care. She felt like she had to kiss Brandon or she'd explode.

She took another step toward him, inhaling his amazing scent—a mix of sweat and his Acqua di Parma deodorant. "I've just been thinking about . . ." she trailed off, glancing up at Brandon through her lashes. "You. A lot."

Brandon ran a hand through his slightly damp hair, and Callie couldn't help herself. She reached up and touched his chin, her hand trembling a little as it met the beard scruff. Before Brandon could say anything, she leaned forward and pressed her lips to his skin, right on his jawbone. He tasted like salt. "Callie . . . I can't do this. I have a girlfriend."

But he didn't step away.

Callie looked up, letting her eyes meet his. "I don't care," she whispered. Butterflies fluttered like crazy in her stomach, and she just couldn't stop herself. She kissed him.

For a moment, he resisted. But then she felt his mouth open against hers, and his hands slide down her sides. She pressed against him, hungrily, and he stumbled backward. Brandon's hands were everywhere, and her lips devoured his neck. It was like he was a drug. And the best part was that she could tell he felt the exact same way.

The two of them spun around and landed with a crash onto his bed. Callie's hands ran up Brandon's back, tearing at his sweaty shirt. She groaned with pleasure. It felt amazing to kiss him again.

"Brandon?"

"Yes, Callie?" Brandon leaned on an elbow, reluctantly taking his lips off hers. He was panting, his heart beating faster than it had in his entire hour on the squash court. Everything happened so quickly—was he really kissing Callie again? He'd been certain those feelings were all dead. But then suddenly everything came rushing back, and it was like they'd never been apart. He gently brushed a strawberry blond lock off her cheek and stared down at her. She was the love of his life, no doubt about that. And, as if by magic, she had somehow realized it.

"No. It's *Hellie*."

Brandon sprang to his feet, straightening his clothes. A moment ago, his whole life was a dream, and now it felt like a nightmare. He stared at his open laptop. There, on his screen, the iChat window was open. Hellie's angry, confused face stared back at him from her dorm room in Switzerland. He didn't even need to ask what she'd seen. She'd clearly seen it all.

Busted.

IsaacDresden: How's the project coming?

JennyHumphrey: I actually just left a Pilates class—I love Jan
Plan!

IsaacDresden: Sorry to spring this on you, but do you
wanna have dinner at my house tomorrow? My
dad personally requested that you come.

JennyHumphrey: What? That sounds terrifying!

IsaacDresden: Nah, he just wants to talk to you about art
some more. He doesn't bite.

JennyHumphrey: Okay, as long as you're there.

IsaacDresden: Where else would I be?

OwlNet   Instant Message Inbox

AlanStGirard: Dude, where are U? U were supposed to meet
                        us in the snack bar at 4.

JulianMcCafferty: Sorry, man. I totally forgot. I'll be right there.

AlanStGirard: R U busy hooking up w/ Tinsley right now?
                        Making her model that hot prom dress again?

AlanStGirard: Or that red bikini?

JulianMcCafferty: Shut the fuck up, all right? I'm on my way.

WildernessMan Log: Heath vs. Wild

Day 49 (feels like)

Woke up to see whole fucking gang of raccoons tearing into my pack.
Fucker from yesterday brought back his whole family. So cold it took me
five minutes to get up and chase them away. Packets of torn jerky with
raccoon cooties lying all over campsite now. Need a shotgun.

Noon temp: Really fucking cold.

Food: Think I can smell the dining hall cooking chocolate chip pancakes.
Delicious. Would love to slather them with butter and sprinkle on some
powdered sugar. Can almost taste them in my mouth.

Warmth: None.

Mood: Thought I saw some skiers again. Or else they were fairies. Wood
nymphs? Someone or something was laughing. I miss girls. They smell so
nice, and their hair is so soft.

AlisonQuentin: They're playing Iron Man on the big screen in Berkman Hall tomorrow night—U wanna go?

JennyHumphrey: Wish I could but I'm having dinner at the dean's.

AlisonQuentin: What? I guess dating the dean's son comes in handy!!

JennyHumphrey: It's not like that . . . Isaac and I are just friends.

AlisonQuentin: Sweetie, I don't judge. Isaac's hot, and I'm totally jealous. Maybe you can get the dean to declare Jan Plan a year-round thing?

JennyHumphrey: I'm just going to try to not make a fool of myself.

AlisonQuentin: Ha! Make sure to have fun playing footsie under the table!

CallieVernon: Hey, stranger. What R U up to? I haven't seen you in days.

TinsleyCarmichael: Been busy with Isla, working on our project.

CallieVernon: What's up w/ Julian? I saw him at lunch, looking like shit.

TinsleyCarmichael: I don't really know. We're not exactly together.

CallieVernon: WHAT? Since when?

TinsleyCarmichael: Since the other day. I dunno.

CallieVernon: Do U want to come up and have margaritas tonight? And talk?

TinsleyCarmichael: Can't. Having dinner at the dean's.

CallieVernon: With Isla, U mean. Have fun.

16

A WAVERLY OWL ASKS NOT WHAT SHE CAN DO FOR WAVERLY—BUT WHAT WAVERLY CAN DO FOR HER.

Jenny spent all of Friday morning in the Waverly Art Museum, which housed a small but respectable collection of early American photography. She'd holed up in the slide library in the basement, clicking through slide after slide of black-and-white photographs. She went through a series of still photos of a racing horse, caught suspended in air midstride. When she clicked through them quickly, it looked like the horse was running in one fluid movement. How cool would it be if all her drawings could merge together, capturing the movement into one piece of art? After three hours crouched in front of a slide projector, Jenny had half a dozen good sketches and an aching lower back. But it felt great.

Now, waking up from a late-afternoon nap in her dorm room, the sky was already darkening. Dinner at the dean's tonight? Thank God Tinsley would be there, too. Now that she was working with Isla, the two of them were practically inseparable. Jenny was grateful for the presence of another non-family member. She felt flattered, and a little nervous, that Isaac had invited her. Was it just to be friendly . . . or did he really want his parents' approval? Their walk in the snow the other night had been romantic, but she was kind of grateful for the groundskeeper's interruption. She was sure Isaac had been about to kiss her—and she wasn't sure that's what she wanted.

Well, of course she did. But not yet. She had a history of jumping into romantic relationships at Waverly, and so far all of them had ended badly. Jenny had fallen for Easy Walsh the first time she saw him crossing the quad in his paint-splattered Levis, carrying a giant sketchbook under his arm. And then there was Julian, who'd made her forget about Easy, but that fizzled quickly as well. She'd been equally crazy about Drew, the hot senior lacrosse guy who turned out only to be interested in one thing—and it wasn't falling in love. She didn't want Isaac to turn into another mistake.

Besides, she'd heard the whispering about her getting special treatment because of her burgeoning friendship with Isaac. She knew that was a huge part of why the dean let her work alone on her art project—but she wanted the favors to end there.

The dean's house stood on top of a small hill near the front gate of campus. It was a stately white Greek Revival building with black shutters and a giant porch held up by enormous

Doric columns. Jenny's heart raced. Ever since she'd first set foot on campus, she'd imagined what it would be like to step into the dean's elegant residence. And here she was, pressing the thumb of her yellow Banana Republic mitten against the doorbell.

A stunning woman in a deep blue-and-green paisley silk wrap dress answered the door. "You must be Jenny. I'm Karina Dresden, Isaac and Isla's mom." She was tall and statuesque, with long reddish-brown hair down her back. Except for some fine lines at the corners of her eyes, her face was perfectly smooth, and Jenny wondered if she had amazing genes or regular access to Botox. "Please, come in."

"Nice to meet you," Jenny squeaked nervously as she followed Mrs. Dresden across the black marble floor of the foyer. The interior of the house was as gorgeous as the exterior, and just as elegant and refined. Two enormous red and orange abstract expressionist paintings hung on the pale gray walls, making Jenny feel like she'd entered another museum. "Those aren't Rothkos, are they?" she asked, her eyes widening.

"Why yes," Mrs. Dresden replied, staring at the paintings fondly. "They've been in the family for ages. We have some other pieces upstairs that I'll have to show you later."

"I'd like that," Jenny managed to say, tearing her eyes off the luminous canvases to take in the rest of the foyer. A wide dark wood staircase wound up to the second floor, and the domed ceiling culminated in a stained glass skylight. It was illuminated from above by the moon, an ethereal glow filling the space. "That's so beautiful!" Jenny exclaimed, forgetting herself and staring up at it like a child.

"It's an incredible house—we're still getting used to it all." Mrs. Dresden smiled as she hung Jenny's coat in the hall closet. Jenny caught a whiff of her perfume, vanilla and some kind of exotic flower. "We're so happy you could join us for dinner."

"Thank you for inviting me." Jenny wiped her clammy palms on her black-and-white houndstooth J. Crew skirt. She'd put it together with a black sateen puffed-sleeve turtleneck, her red ballet flats sparkling under the light of a chandelier. While she wanted to look sweet and friendly for Isaac's parents, she didn't want to look boring for him. "It's nice to have a dinner outside of the dining hall every once in a while."

"Oh, you might be missing out, 'cause I heard it was sloppy joe night." Isaac appeared, grinning, in the doorway to the living room, and Jenny felt her cheeks heat just at the sight of him. He had on a navy blue long-sleeved Lacoste polo shirt, gray corduroys, and a pair of distressed brown leather loafers. He touched her lightly on the back. "Thanks for coming."

"Join the other kids in the sitting room, Jenny. I'm just going to check on the cook." Mrs. Dresden steered Isaac and Jenny into the slate-blue-walled living room, where a Charlie Parker saxophone recording was playing through the surround-sound system. Tinsley, in a gold silk tie-front Twelfth Street by Cynthia Vincent dress, waved at Jenny, looking perfectly at home in the dean's living room. She swirled a wineglass full of what looked like cola and leaned back on the velvet chaise lounge that stretched in front of the enormous brick fireplace. A brilliant fire crackled.

"What a beautiful fire," Jenny exclaimed, then immediately blushed. She knew she sounded like a twelve-year-old at Christmas.

"You know Tinsley, of course. And this is my sister, Isla." Isaac swept his arm out toward his sister, who sat on the red velvet piano bench, leaning back against the keys of a gorgeous black baby grand. A narrow vase of white tulips sat in the middle of the polished black top. "You guys haven't met yet, right?"

Isla stood up to shake Jenny's hand. Jenny had seen her from far away, but up close, she looked like a more feminine version of Isaac—the same wavy, almost-black hair, same pale green eyes, same high cheekbones. "Nice to meet you, Jenny." In a pair of bell-bottom black satin pants and an angelic-looking white lacy Gold Hawk top, she looked sweeter than Jenny had imagined. But there was also a glint in her eye, like she knew all kinds of secrets and wasn't about to tell you any of them. No wonder she and Tinsley got along so well.

"You, too." Jenny glanced at Isaac, wishing he'd put his arm around her again. "Welcome to Waverly."

"Thanks." Isla laughed. Turquoise teardrop earrings dangled from her earlobes. "I just hope it can handle me."

"Few places can." Isaac rolled his eyes. Jenny wondered what that was all about. She hadn't gotten a sense yet if Isaac and Isla were close. "Jenny, can I get you something to drink? Soda or water?"

"I'm fine, thanks."

Tinsley got to her feet, wobbling slightly on her black leather L.A.M.B. pumps. Something about her smile seemed a little forced to Jenny. Her eyes were a little more made-up than normal, and a little reddened, as if she'd been crying. Or smoking pot. She'd heard that Tinsley and Julian had broken up, but hadn't believed it. Now, she wasn't so sure. "Isla has some Bacardi in her room, if you'd like it," she whispered to Jenny.

"Thanks, but I'm good." Jenny shook her head, her braid swishing against her back. "Where's your dad?" she asked, glancing up at Isaac.

"He's the chef," Isaac replied, his piercing green eyes focused on Jenny's face. "And he really gets into it, so be sure to compliment the food profusely."

"Dinner is served!" Dean Dresden announced, appearing in the doorway with Mrs. Dresden's arm linked through his. He had on a white apron and a white puffy chef's hat and was holding a wooden spoon into the air. He looked like a middle-aged *Top Chef* wannabe, albeit one with a supermodel on his arm. Jenny giggled. It was so weird to see the handsome, distinguished-looking dean in his own home—he was surprisingly silly. "I hope you kids are hungry."

"Daddy!" Isla cried as they filed into the dining room. The antique cherrywood table was set with six funky yellow square plates set on bamboo place mats. "Take off your apron. We have guests."

"Of course, sweetie." The dean pulled off his splattered apron and smoothed down his royal blue button-down—no tie, top button open. He kissed Isla on the forehead and smiled at Jenny. The chef's hat still sat on his head, until Isla reached up and plucked it off. "Jenny. Nice to see you again. Please, everyone. Sit down."

"The salad looks delicious, Dean Dresden." Tinsley passed the wooden salad bowl to Jenny. The dean and his wife were seated at the long ends of the table, with Isaac and Jenny on one side and Tinsley and Isla on the other. Jenny scooped some arugula onto her plate with the giant wooden forks. A tiny cherry tomato rolled off her plate.

"Thank you, Tinsley. And thank you girls for coming. It's a pleasure to get to spend some time with Isaac and Isla's new friends." Mrs. Dresden leaned over the table, pouring ice water into everyone's glasses. "I think this whole—what do they call it? Jan Plan?—thing sounds wonderful. We haven't seen that at any of the other schools."

"It *is* fun," Isla spoke up, forking diced cucumber into her mouth. "Tinsley and I have been working really hard." She winked at Tinsley.

"I wish you'd tell us about your project, sweetie," Mrs. Dresden admonished as she sat back in her chair. She touched her dangling silver necklace, nestled comfortably in her cleavage. Jenny couldn't help wondering what Heath Ferro would do if he were here, having dinner with the dean's gorgeous wife instead of living out in the wilderness. Heath was always talking about having a thing for older women. Of course, he had a thing for *younger* women, too.

"You'll see soon enough." Isla pressed her lips together mysteriously.

"And how is your artwork going, Jenny?" Isaac asked, his green eyes shifting toward her. "Jenny's studying the effects of movement," Isaac explained to the rest of the table. "Right?"

"Yes." Jenny smiled at Isaac. "I've been doing a lot of sketching, and a lot of people watching." As she took a sip of water and looked at the dean and his family's friendly faces across the candlelit table, she realized how lucky she was. Here she was, sitting in the dean's dining room, enjoying his homemade cooking, talking to him like he was a normal person. "And it's been great so far."

"Good." Dean Dresden set down his fork, a playful look on his face. "And do you girls have any words of advice for me, as I take over the helm? Any suggestions?"

"Well," Tinsley said innocently, pushing her dark pin-straight hair behind her ears. Tiny diamond studs glittered in her earlobes. "Since you're asking, is there anything you can do about the Latin requirement?" She smiled sweetly.

Jenny giggled. She hadn't expected to feel so relaxed here. "What if everyone could take a schoolwide field trip? A weekend in New York or Boston."

"It sounds like it could be very school-spirit-building, Dad." Isaac laughed, buttering a warm whole wheat roll. "You're always talking about school spirit."

"That's definitely true," Dean Dresden admitted, chewing thoughtfully. "You know how I love school spirit."

Isla glanced at her mother and they both rolled their eyes, making the rest of the table laugh. "Yes, because you never shut up about it," she pointed out, sweetly.

"Or what about letting sophomores have singles?" Jenny suggested, getting into the spirit.

"But what about you, sir—how are you enjoying your time at Waverly?" Tinsley leaned forward, smiling politely. Jenny was always a little in awe of how comfortable Tinsley was talking to adults.

"Very much, thanks for asking." The dean chuckled. "Except I have yet to meet most of the faculty. I'm hosting a little get-to-know-you faculty dinner on Saturday night, in fact, where I'll get to meet most of them for the first time."

"At Le Petit Coq?" Jenny asked, mentioning the French restaurant in town where anyone requiring a fancier locale than the pizza place in downtown Rhinecliff usually wound up. She'd never been there—when her father visited, he was more interested in the pineapple-and-ham pizza at Ritoli's than in escargot. But it was the kind of restaurant where people lingered for hours over five-course meals and bottles of expensive red wine.

"Yes," Mrs. Dresden spoke up, pressing her hand to her ample chest. "I hear they have an amazing Parisian chef who makes a duck à l'orange that is to die for. That's my favorite."

"My dear, the asparagus-and-pine-nut risotto I have for you tonight is going to make you forget all about French cuisine." Dean Dresden pushed his chair back and disappeared into the kitchen.

While Mrs. Dresden chatted with Tinsley about the shops in downtown Rhinecliff, Jenny took the opportunity to lean closer to Isaac, an idea forming. "Your parents are going to be out on Saturday night. How cool would it be to throw a little party here?" she whispered. She knew it was a risky proposition, but she was in a daring mood. Why not have a little fun?

"You have a devious mind," Isaac whispered back, raising an eyebrow. "I like it."

Jenny grinned and stabbed a cherry tomato with her fork. When a Waverly Owl sees an opportunity, shouldn't she take advantage of it?

AlisonQuentin: U want to hear something strange? I kind of miss pervy Heath!

JennyHumphrey: I know! It just seems kind of quiet without him.

AlisonQuentin: Alan said he saw some bloody rabbit tracks out past the soccer fields. Do you really think Heath's eating bunnies?

JennyHumphrey: Ew. But I did see some smoke coming from the woods today. I never knew he was a chef!

17

A WAVERLY OWL NEVER KISSES AND TELLS.

"Whoa." Sebastian let out a low growl when he opened the door to his dorm room. Brett was standing there in her cropped leather Fendi jacket over her emerald green silk spaghetti-strap Betsey Johnson dress. The dress set off her catlike green eyes and porcelain skin to perfection. In her four-inch Stuart Weitzman peep-toe patent leather pumps, she was almost at Sebastian's eye level. "You look incredible. Are you sure we're just going to the movies?"

Brett grinned despite herself. She twisted the ends of the patterned silk Hermès scarf her mother gave her for Christmas around her wrist. "I just wanted to look nice."

That wasn't quite true. The revelation that Chrissy had dated Sebastian was like a wake-up call. With Jeremiah Mortimer, Brett's previous—and only other—boyfriend, it had been so much easier. He went to St. Lucius Academy, fifteen miles away, and it didn't matter who he'd dated since Brett

didn't need to face his exes all the time. The one time she'd
run into an ex of Jeremiah's at a Waverly party had ended in
complete disaster.

The situation with Sebastian wasn't at that level of hor-
ror just yet—but it was strange, nonetheless. She hadn't even
known Sebastian before she started to tutor him over the fall.
He mostly hung out with seniors, potheads, and slackers, and
while his crowd had occasionally crossed paths with Brett's,
it wasn't like they knew all the gossip about each other. And
so Brett had no idea who he'd dated—or at least, she *hadn't*,
until yesterday, when she'd followed up Benny's suggestion and
met with Devon Sprague. Devon, a blond senior girl on Brett's
varsity field hockey team, kept a file on her laptop chronicling
every rumored Waverly relationship, hookup, flirtation, and
everything in between. A discreet chat at CoffeeRoasters was
all it took for Brett to learn that in the past year alone Sebastian had managed to "date"—she used the word loosely—the
following girls, in addition to Chrissy and Alexis: Leila Rodriguez, a pretty art student who'd been accepted early to RISD;
Molly Theal, a slutty blond softball player who was notorious
for taking her clothes off at Waverly parties; and the overly tat-
tooed Leigh Nissonson, who made the pre–Brad Pitt Angelina
Jolie look sane.

"You okay?" Sebastian asked, stepping back and taking
Brett's chin in his hand, his strong fingers warm against her
cold skin. His dark eyes, almost black, were so wide and car-
ing, how could she doubt him? "You look like you just spaced
out."

Brett smiled weakly. He was so handsome, in a simple white button-down that set off his olive skin and a pair of dark-rinse Levis. But how many girls had stood right here in his doorway and thought the exact same thing? Had Leila Rodriguez sprawled out half naked on his bed while he told her how beautiful she was? Had Molly Theal admired the cheesy Italian flag that took up half his wall?

Brett smoothed her dress out over her knees and tried not to think about it. Why did she even care whom he'd been with? He was with her now. "I'm fine."

"I'm just going to grab my keys from this dude upstairs." Sebastian opened the door.

"This dude upstairs?" Brett repeated, grinning. "You lent your beloved Mustang to some guy whose name you don't even know?"

Sebastian shrugged his shoulders, a bewildered expression on his face. "I think it's Mike. Or Ike. Something like that." He kissed her on the forehead.

"I doubt there's an Ike who goes to school here," she teased.

Sebastian shook his head in mock outrage as he walked out the door. "I'll be back to deal with you in a minute."

She loved watching him walk—it was more of a swagger, really, and when she first met him it had annoyed her. Just another overly confident Waverly player, she thought. But once she got to know him, she discovered he was just comfortable in his skin. He didn't worry about being from tacky New Jersey; he was, in fact, proud that he came from the Garden State and that his father owned a lucrative chain of car dealerships across the tristate area. Unlike Brett, who had for years told people her father was a surgeon, omitting the "plastic" part of his job description out of embarrassment.

Brett got to her feet, the heels of her black pumps clicking against the hardwood floor. With Sebastian gone, she had an incredible urge to look through his stuff. Not to find evidence of other girls, of course—but just to prove to herself that there wasn't any. She quickly opened his desk drawers, searching for mementos of girlfriends past. Since the postcard in Chrissy's room did come from him, she wanted to see if he kept any post-cards from girls. But the only things on Sebastian's walls were his enormous Italian flag, and a giant poster of *The Godfather*.

She opened the long, narrow pencil drawer, and her heart skipped a beat when she saw a stack of pictures. The one on top was of Sebastian having a snowball fight with a girl in a pink puffy coat. Brett looked closer. Wait, that was *her*. It was taken over break, in front of Sebastian's dad's house. His father must have taken the shot without Brett knowing. She smiled, remembering how she'd tackled Sebastian from behind and pushed him into the snow. He kept this in the top of his drawer? That was so sweet.

A knock at the door made her jump. She quickly dropped the picture back into the drawer and closed it guiltily. But when she opened the door there stood Tricia Rieken, wearing a pair of red stilettos, tight black jeans, and a tight black Ed Hardy tank top that showed off her huge chest. Brett had always suspected the rumor about her boob job was false, but when presented with her balloonlike breasts practically popping in her face, she had to admit the rumor seemed awfully valid.

"Yes?" Brett asked coolly, crossing her arms over her own chest. She'd hated Tricia ever since freshman year, when she'd flirted her way to an A in Monsieur Lamont's French class—an A that Brett had to earn.

"Just looking for Seb." Tricia peered over Brett's shoulder, as if Brett were hiding him. Then her heavily mascaraed eyes lasered in on Brett. "We hang out every Friday night."

Hang out? From Tricia's outfit, it was obvious she hadn't come over to play board games. "Guess you'll have to find something else to do," Brett replied sharply, slamming the door in Tricia's face.

She slid into Sebastian's desk chair. What the hell? Okay, so not only had Sebastian hooked up with half the females at Waverly, he also had a regular Friday night booty call with one of the skankiest. How could a guy even *like* someone like Tricia Rieken? She was all boobs and no personality.

The door opened again and Sebastian came in. His hair was flopping sexily over his eyes, but Brett was too annoyed to think it was cute.

"You missed *Tricia*," Brett announced. "If I'd known you had a regular date on Friday nights, we could have seen the movie some other time."

"Oh, shit." Sebastian rubbed his forehead, a chagrined look in his eyes. "I forgot about Tricia."

"You *forgot* about her? About the *skanky* girl you hook up with every week?" Brett sprang to her feet, too irritated to sit still. When her mother got angry, she always paced back and forth across the room, flailing her arms. Brett had to squeeze her arms to her sides to keep from doing the same. Maybe it was genetic. "What about Leila? And Alena? And *Chrissy*? Did you forget about them, too?"

"Brett, what are you talking about?" The familiar amused gleam lit up Sebastian's eyes. "You can't be jealous of girls I was with before I met you."

"Maybe I wouldn't be, if there were, like, two or three." Brett twisted her scarf tightly around her finger, accidentally snagging the delicate fabric with her chunky rose coral ring. "But I can't even count them all!"

"Calm down, okay?"

Her voice softened as she looked out the window. "Am I just the next one?"

"No!" Sebastian's face darkened. She felt him step closer behind her, and she almost jumped when his strong hands grabbed her waist. He breathed into her hair. "Look, all those girls are in the past. I don't do that anymore."

Brett turned to face him. "So . . . what am I?"

"You're my future." His mouth curled up at the corner, hesitantly, as if afraid of sounding cheesy. But her heart melted. Okay, so it kind of sounded like a line, but it was also ridiculously sweet. And she could tell he meant it. No one had told her she was his future before.

"I guess that's all right, then," Brett replied, stepping into his arms. She tenderly wiped the lock of hair off his forehead with her finger, planting her lips in the same spot. His hands slid up and down her sides, and a warm feeling coursed through her body.

How could she care about stupid Tricia Rieken when she had *this?*

"We'd better get going if we want to make the movie," Sebastian murmured into Brett's ear. He kissed her on the cheek, just inches from her lips.

Brett closed her eyes. "Let's make the later show."

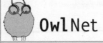

OwlNet   Instant Message Inbox

BennyCunningham: You're working w/ Julian on some movie for Jan Plan, right?

AlanStGirard: Let me guess, you want to know if we saved U a part. You're in luck—we do have a small, topless role I think you'd be perfect for.

BennyCunningham: Thanks but no thanks. Just wanted to know if it's true about him and Tinsley.

AlanStGirard: That they're kaput? Fraid so. But don't even think about it—he's not your type.

BennyCunningham: Freshmen are not for me. Dean's sons are more my type.

AlanStGirard: Too bad Isaac's with Jenny.

BennyCunningham: That's just a dirty rumor!

AlanStGirard: Dunno. Heard she had dinner at his house tonight.

BennyCunningham: That could mean anything!

A WAVERLY OWL SOMETIMES FINDS SATISFACTION
IN CULTIVATING THE ENVY OF OTHERS.

"You ready?" Isla asked, nudging a bare elbow into Tinsley's waist. It was Saturday morning, and Tinsley was dressed in a strapless pink Alice + Olivia micromini cocktail dress. Her manicured cherry-colored toenails peeped sexily out of a pair of sky-high gold Jimmy Choos. Probably not the most appropriate outfit for the gym, but it was just right for their photography project.

"Of course." Tinsley smiled, pushing through the double doors into the main room of the Waverly Athletic Club. Late Saturday mornings were one of the busiest times, with everyone eager to work off their Friday night pizza-and-beer binges. She and Isla had chosen to stage their latest photo shoot for precisely that reason. Isla had borrowed Tinsley's body-hugging red Alexander Wang minidress and a pair of black sandals that laced up her calves. "The question is, are they ready for us?"

Isla giggled. The sound of some terrible Britney Spears song pulsed through the sound system. Did people really think bad music made you work out harder? "That's what I like about you, Tinsley Carmichael. You're always up for something new."

Tinsley sighed. *New* was right. She still couldn't quite believe she'd broken up with Julian. When she'd gone to his room Wednesday night, she was more than a little drunk and hadn't meant to do anything drastic. She was sure he'd call or e-mail the next day, but she hadn't heard a word from him since. Well, screw him.

He just didn't *get* her. Tinsley shuddered, even though the gym was overheated.

She thought it would take a moment for people to look up from their workouts to notice her and Isla, but in about ten seconds, Tinsley felt the eyes of everyone in the gym on them. She tossed her loose hair over her bare shoulder, letting it fall into shimmery waves and tickle her skin.

"Let's do weights first. Over there." Isla pointed a bright red fingernail toward the weight machines, crowded with tall, sweaty Waverly guys in long basketball shorts and faded T-shirts that clung to their chests.

"Do you mind if we use this bench?" Tinsley asked politely as Parker DuBois, the quiet senior from Belgium or France or somewhere in Western Europe, dropped a set of barbells onto the giant rack with a clank.

Parker almost jumped in surprise. His handsome face flushed at the sight of two pretty girls in minuscule dresses and towering heels. A funny grin flashed across his face. Parker was so shy with girls, rumors always flew about whether or not he was gay. But Tinsley knew from the way he stared at her bare legs that he was far from interested in men. "Uh, help yourselves," he said, in a slightly accented voice. He pushed his blond hair off his forehead and retreated to a butterfly machine in the corner—coincidentally, with an unobstructed view of the girls.

"Do you girls need any help?" Lon Baruzza, in a wifebeater that revealed his cut biceps, appeared next to Tinsley and Isla, grinning eagerly.

"I can hold your camera if you two want, you know, any shots together." Chris Avery, the six-foot-four star forward of the basketball team, offered.

Isla shot them a cool look. "Thanks, but we can handle it, boys."

Tinsley laughed and held the camera up, clicking off a few shots. She loved Isla's attitude—it was like she didn't give a shit about anyone, and it just made everyone want to be with her so much *more*. Even though Isla was only a year ahead of Tinsley, she seemed much older. Tinsley had asked Isla a few questions about her past, but Isla always brushed them off. And, as Tinsley wasn't one to pry, she let it go. She definitely understood that the element of mystery only added to a person's intrigue.

"Your turn." Isla grabbed the camera and focused it on Tinsley, who picked up two barbells. She was in great shape because of the demanding tennis workouts her coach designed for the whole team. Even in the off season, Ms. Nemerov, who'd played tennis for Russia in the Barcelona Olympics, assigned each girl on her tennis team a specialized workout regimen. Tinsley had no problem sticking to hers.

She raised the slim five-pound weights, pushing them up in an artful shoulder press. Suddenly, with her flexed, toned arms lifting toward the sky, Tinsley felt like a goddess. She could feel Lon and the other boys staring at her body, and out of the corner of her eye she saw Sage Francis and Rifat Jones huffing away on StairMasters, wearing sweaty old T-shirts and saggy Waverly shorts. Their eyes were positively dripping with envy. Tinsley felt her lips curl into a smile as she heard a couple of camera phones snapping away at her. *Go ahead*, she thought. *Tell your friends*.

Tinsley Carmichael was back.

OwlNet　　　　　　　　　　　　Instant Message Inbox

SageFrancis:　Just found an invite under my door to a party at the dean's tonite—did U get one, too?

RyanReynolds:　Yup. Sounds sweet. Who do U think is behind it?

SageFrancis:　Isla and Tinsley, I bet.

RyanReynolds:　Dunno. I saw Jenny and the dude looking all chummy over coffee this morning.

SageFrancis:　They were together again? Damn, she's not giving anyone else a crack at him!

19

A WAVERLY OWL BELIEVES IN SECOND CHANCES.

Saturday afternoon, Brandon skipped lunch and hiked into town to pick up flowers for Callie. It was a sunny, mild winter day, and the streets of Rhinecliff were bustling with activity—families pushing baby strollers, young couples holding hands, an ancient-looking man and woman kissing on a park bench. Brandon felt like he'd been walking on air ever since he and Callie had kissed. Suddenly everything seemed to make sense again.

Well, not everything. He rubbed his hand over his face as he thought about Hellie. After calling her every hour the other day, she'd finally picked up. He apologized profusely, but she didn't really want to hear it. No one deserved to have to watch her boyfriend cheat on her, long distance, over iChat.

But he would never take back what had happened with Callie, not for anything in the world. He'd always known they were destined to be together. He just wished that Hellie hadn't seen it. But he and Callie were in love again, and Hellie was better off without him.

Carrying a gorgeous bouquet of orchids, he pushed through the door to the rare books library. They were scheduled to tape the last interview with Brett, who hadn't been able to make it to the Atrium the other day.

He spotted Callie leaning over the video camera. She sneezed, and Brandon smiled. He'd forgotten how cute her little sneezes were—he imagined a bunny sneezing would sound like that.

Unable to resist, Brandon walked up behind her and planted a kiss on the nape of her neck. The long wavy strawberry blond ponytail tickled his face. He could feel her body shiver with pleasure before she spun around.

The smile on her face disappeared as she saw the flowers Brandon was holding. "Oh . . ." she trailed off. In her plaid Emilio Pucci jumper and her mustard yellow flats, she didn't exactly look like the kind of girl who'd have a frantic, hair-pulling, clothes-tearing makeout session on an ex-boyfriend's bed in front of his current girlfriend.

"They're for you," Brandon said, suddenly nervous. Was yesterday some sort of hallucination? Had Callie not been nibbling on his neck and digging her nails into his back? No, he'd seen the scratch marks in the mirror that morning. At least he wasn't crazy. But why wouldn't she want flowers? Didn't girls always want flowers? "I just wanted to, you know. Give you something nice."

Callie stared at the bouquet of lavender and white flowers

and took a deep breath. They were gorgeous, and it was sweet. But . . . she already knew the sweet Brandon. He wasn't the one who wanted to make her tear his clothes off. That was the aloof Brandon who had a girlfriend, and who didn't really care about Callie. Their frantic makeout session yesterday had been completely hot, and she was already wondering when they'd get the chance to do it again.

But Brandon didn't think that they were a couple now, did he? They'd already tried that once, and it didn't work. And now, after one hookup, he was bringing her flowers?

Before she could ask, Brett strolled through the door, wearing a yellow slouchy C&C California sweater and a pair of skinny gray jeans tucked into fleece-lined suede boots. Her bright red hair was twisted up and held in place by half a dozen tiny butterfly clips. "Am I late?"

"Not at all." Callie rushed over to Brett, grateful for her friend's interruption. "Thanks so much for doing this."

Brett smiled and waved a hand in the air, then frowned slightly at the camera. "I didn't know you were videotaping this." She touched her hair.

"Don't worry, you look great. And I'm . . ." She glanced at Brandon. "Er, we're just using the video to make the interviewing easier. No one's going to see it. Come over here. Sit in front of the camera, okay?" Callie shuttled Brett into a leather-backed armchair. Brandon turned the camera on her, and Callie sank back into the chair next to it, crossing her legs. She could feel Brandon's eyes on her short jumper, and her annoyance toward him softened. It wasn't so bad that he wanted to bring her flowers—it was sweet, after all. As long as he didn't expect too much.

Callie shuffled through her index cards. "I'm just going to ask you a bunch of questions, and try to be as honest as possible." Brett nodded, leaning back into the chair and staring up at the vaulted ceiling. "Have you ever been in love?"

Brett nodded her head slowly. "Yes."

"More than once?"

Brett nodded again. "Twice."

Callie's lips twisted in surprise. *Twice?* Brett was in love with Sebastian—already? She'd been madly in love with Jeremiah Mortimer, her long-haired football star boyfriend, for what seemed like forever. How had she managed to move on so quickly? Callie leaned forward in her chair. She really wanted to know. "How did you know it was love?"

"I don't know." Brett shifted in her seat. She tapped her glittery pink fingernails against the padded leather arm of the chair. "It was different each time."

"Do you believe in true love?"

"I don't really think I know what that means. I mean, I fell in love with Jeremiah, and I was sure he was my true love. You know, the one I'd been waiting for and all that." She shrugged and smiled at Callie. "But there were just so many ups and downs. Like, we were always fighting—always misunderstanding each other. It was like we were . . . I don't know. Speaking different languages or something."

Immediately, Callie thought about her tumultuous

relationship with Easy. They'd broken up about eight hundred times. There were plenty of ups, of course . . . but they always seemed to be followed by an even bigger down. And even though the making-up part of fighting was really, really fun, the fighting part sucked. Just this September, Easy had broken up with her to date Jenny, her *roommate*. Talk about a down. That made Callie want to drive a sharpened pencil into someone's eye.

"And now, with Sebastian . . ." Brett bit her lip to keep from smiling. Her cheeks colored a little. "It's not what I expected, but it's amazing." She absentmindedly touched her cheek, and something about the gesture told Callie that she was thinking about Sebastian, about how he kissed her.

"Do you believe in soul mates?"

Brett tilted her head to the side. "Yes and no. I believe we connect with people in different ways—and sometimes it's not the kind of person you thought it was, but it's so much better." She shrugged. "I mean, I think everyone's always going to have a special place in their heart for their first love—you know, the one who made them realize what love is and all that. But I don't think that means you can't find it again—or something better."

Callie found herself nodding in agreement. She glanced over at Brandon, who was watching Brett through the video camera. In profile, he looked so serious. Then, as if he felt Callie's eyes on him, he looked up. The moment their eyes met, Callie felt a connection.

Brett had told her everything she needed to know. *People can have more than one love.* And maybe, just maybe, here was the first sign that she wasn't doomed post-Easy.

Brandon smiled back at her, a curious half-smile that made heat rush to Callie's cheeks. She didn't know exactly what this was between them, but she'd never know if she didn't give it a real chance.

AlanStGirard: U going to the party at the dean's house?

BennyCunningham: Hell, yeah. I wanna make a move on that hot son.

AlanStGirard: Mmm, might have to move fast. Heard he likes Jenny. And they're behind the party. Sounds like it's serious.

BennyCunningham: He just hasn't met me yet!

AlanStGirard: Don't worry, I'll be there to console you when it doesn't work out.

OwlNet

LonBaruzza: U know that fantasy I've always had about doing it on Dean Marymount's bed?

RyanReynolds: Yeah, and it's pretty sick. Plus, I bet he took his bed with him.

LonBaruzza: I'm willing to break in the new dean's bed. Think his daughter's up for it? She seems wild.

RyanReynolds: Dunno. Can't hurt to make an offer.

A WAVERLY OWL KNOWS HOW TO BE A GOOD HOSTESS.

Jenny Humphrey opened the stainless steel Sub-Zero freezer in the Dresdens' state-of-the-art kitchen and grabbed a plastic bag full of cubed ice. The sounds of laughter and clinking glasses filtered in from the living room, which was filled with happy Waverly Owls, relaxing and lounging on the dean's furniture. The party was a huge success. That morning, she and Isaac had typed up invitations and slunk around campus, trying to slide them beneath dorm room doors without anyone seeing them. It was fun, and strangely romantic—Jenny felt kind of like Harriet the Spy, with an extremely sexy accomplice. They'd kept the guest list on the smaller side, hoping it would make the cleanup go faster when the evening came to an end.

She poured a bag of ice into a crystal bowl from the Dresdens' pantry, then used the knife to slide the chopped kiwi, oranges, and apples from the cutting board into the bowl. The sounds of an old Coldplay song spilled through the surround-sound speakers.

"Wow. You make a mean sangria." Isaac appeared at her side, wearing a charcoal gray Ralph Lauren T-shirt and a pair of dark wool Theory trousers. Around his neck, she glimpsed the edge of a braided leather rope necklace that looked vaguely African. She'd noticed it the other day—it looked like the kind of necklace a girlfriend would give.

"I like your necklace," she said, hoping it would prompt him to say more. She didn't know exactly what was going on between the two of them. Was it weird that they hadn't kissed yet? Did that mean he wasn't attracted to her?

Isaac looked surprised. He touched his necklace, as if trying to remember what it was. "Oh, that. Isla brought it back from Senegal."

"Senegal? When was she there?" Jenny asked, leaning back against the counter. It sounded so exotic for a high school girl to visit Senegal. Jenny wasn't even sure exactly where it was, or what language they spoke.

"This fall. She, uh, sort of spent the semester there." Isaac grabbed a grape and popped it into his mouth.

"Really?" Jenny asked, her eyes widening. "That's cool."

Isaac shrugged. "Kind of. My parents really encouraged her to go." He fingered his necklace absentmindedly. "There was this incident."

"Now it's getting juicy," Jenny teased, leaning closer to Isaac. "You've got to tell me the whole story."

He laughed. "It's not that exciting. Isla's just always been kind of, as my parents call it, high-spirited. Last spring, she got kind of close to this one teacher. Male. Young. Kind of looked like Brad Pitt."

"Oh, my," Jenny said, then immediately blushed. She sounded like a granny.

"I don't know exactly what happened, but basically the teacher came forward and told my dad that Isla was, uh, trying to cross certain boundaries. Isla said it was exactly the opposite." Isaac reached up and tapped his fingers against a copper pan hanging over the counter. "So, the teacher was fired. And Isla . . . well, it kind of worked out for her. The story was everywhere, so my parents let her take a semester abroad, something she'd been begging to do all along."

"Wow." Jenny bit her lip. She loved secrets, but mostly she was happy that Isaac was sharing them with *her*. That had to mean something, right? "I won't tell anyone. Promise."

"I trust you." Isaac grinned at her. She noticed for the first time that one of his bottom teeth had a tiny chip in it. It was adorable.

Sage Francis rushed in, wearing a slinky black dress. "We need more sangria in the library. We're starting a game of Twister." She ignored Jenny and batted her glitter-covered eyelids at Isaac.

"Coming right up," Isaac announced, barely glancing at Sage as he expertly popped the cork on a bottle of Bordeaux from the dean's extensive wine cellar and poured the wine into the crystal bowl. He'd brought Jenny down there earlier, to help pick some mediocre-looking wines that wouldn't be missed. She was still thinking about how nice it had been, just the two of them, in the dimly lit cellar. It would have been the perfect place for a first kiss—but it hadn't happened.

Jenny handed the sangria bowl to Sage. "Nice dress," Sage said, petulantly. Jenny glanced down at her eggplant-colored scoop-neck knit dress from Urban Outfitters, which revealed just the right amount of skin. She touched her hair, smelling of her Frédéric Fekkai Luscious Curls Cream. She could feel it tumbling over her shoulders in long, loose curls, exactly as she'd intended it to.

"Thanks," she said self-consciously, touching the neckline.

The doorbell chimed, an elegant *ding-dong*. "I'll get it," Jenny announced, dashing through the dining room to the foyer, where the expansive black marble floor had been claimed as the dance floor. She and Isaac had lined the stairs with tiny glass tea lights—a fire hazard, to be sure, but the effect was ghostly and romantic. The only other light in the room came from the full moon, beaming through the intricate floral design of the stained glass skylight. She elbowed past a few slow-dancing couples and threw the door open. Callie and Brandon stood on the doorstep, kissing.

"Hello," Jenny said, surprised, as she ushered them into the house. Brandon helped Callie out of her coat. She looked gorgeous and happy, her hazel eyes lined with thick gray kohl that matched her flowing dress. Were they together? Jenny tried to catch her roommate's eye. They'd been all flirty at the Atrium the other day, but Callie hadn't mentioned it again. "Let me take your coats."

"Thanks," Callie mumbled. Even in the dim light, Jenny could tell she was blushing. Jenny grabbed their coats and hung them in the already-stuffed coat closet off to the side of the entryway.

"This is incredible," Brandon noted, staring up at the ceiling of the foyer. His hand rested against Callie's lower back. "It's so romantic." Jenny thought she noticed Callie stepping a little closer to him.

"Hey, do you guys know Isaac?" Jenny spotted him coming out of the dining room. She quickly grabbed him by the sleeve and tugged him over to her friends. "Isaac, this is my roommate Callie, and . . . Brandon." Isaac shook their hands politely. Both her friends sized him up and gave Jenny slight nods of approval.

Jenny's face warmed. "I'm going to change the CD. Put on something better to dance to." Isaac touched her waist as she passed, letting his hand linger a moment.

"You remember how to do it?" he asked. The house was equipped with a surround-sound stereo system, and he'd spent ten minutes showing Jenny how to operate the fancy, four-hundred-CD changer.

"Hopefully I can manage to avoid your mom's John Denver albums." Jenny grinned shyly. The door opened again, and all the flames on the candles flickered, making the shadows on the walls dance. "But as this party's host, you've got to get out on the dance floor."

Isaac groaned. "You haven't seen me dance yet."

"And I'm not leaving until I do," Jenny challenged,

sticking her chin out flirtatiously. She hadn't even noticed that Callie and Brandon had disappeared into another room. When Isaac was around, it was so hard to concentrate on anything else.

"I could deal with that." Isaac laughed, watching Jenny's expression. She could tell already that he liked to make her blush. He was cute, and it had been strangely romantic setting up his house for the party. The candles, the chopping fruit for sangria, the wine-choosing, the stereo instruction. They'd spent hours alone together already.

So why hadn't he kissed her?

Maybe he was waiting for her to kiss him. Flustered by the thought, she pushed her hair out of her flushed face as she strode toward the sound-system control panel in the living room. The click of her stacked-heel boots was drowned out by the sound of the music. She picked up an abandoned wineglass off a bookshelf of rare first editions and set it down on the elegant nineteenth-century end table that they'd carefully covered with a red linen tablecloth.

"Wow, Jenny. I can't believe you guys are throwing a party at the dean's. This is legendary." Evelyn Dahlie patted Jenny on the shoulder as Jenny opened the stereo cabinet and pushed some buttons. Instantly, the music switched to the party mix Jenny had burned that afternoon.

Benny, wearing a clingy lemon yellow Roberto Rodriguez halter top, elbowed Evelyn out of the way. She lowered her voice and whispered into Jenny's ear, her breath boozy. "What's with you and Isaac?"

Sage stepped forward, a slight pout on her bee-stung lips. "You guys looked all cute and stuff in the kitchen."

"I don't know," Jenny answered. And she really didn't. But she did know that it was fun to have people talking about her. Although it did make her a little nervous. Isaac was almost too good-looking for her, and being the new dean's son, he was so high-profile. Was everyone snickering behind her back because she was this little sophomore thinking she had a chance with the new most eligible bachelor on campus?

"Good," Benny replied, rubbing her hands together. "That means he's still up for grabs then."

At that moment, the girls looked up. In the doorway to the foyer, Alan St. Girard and Ryan Reynolds were standing in a cluster with Isaac. And Isaac was looking straight at Jenny.

Benny nudged Jenny a little too hard in the side. "He's staring at you," she hissed.

Jenny blushed, for the millionth time that night. At least she knew she wasn't imagining it.

Brett leaned back against the velvet aqua chaise lounge in the front parlor of the dean's house, her legs crossed in front of her, watching as Benny and Sage hovered around Jenny. They were relentless once they caught the scent of some juicy gossip.

But she was far too comfortable to move. Sebastian, sitting at her feet, was tracing a finger up and down her black-stockinged legs. She felt glamorous in her royal blue Antik Batik silk chiffon hippie dress with its embroidered hemline, and something about sitting in a chaise lounge always made her feel like

Cleopatra. It was hard to imagine that just a few days ago she was upset about losing the *Vogue* internship. If she were in New York right now, she wouldn't be with this gorgeous guy who adored her. You lose some, and you definitely win some.

Sebastian leaned forward and kissed Brett gently on the lips. With his longish black hair and his tightish black T-shirt, he looked like a young Johnny Depp. "Come on . . . you know you want to go upstairs and check out where Marymount used to polish his bald head."

"Is that how you're going to try and lure me upstairs?" Brett asked, in mock incredulity. "That's the worst come-on I've ever heard."

"I guess you haven't had enough sangria yet." Sebastian picked up her empty glass and stood up, shaking his head in disbelief. "'Cause a line of that caliber usually works."

"Maybe on your other girlfriends," Brett joked. Ever since their conversation the other night, after Tricia showed up at Sebastian's door, things between them had been better than ever. She didn't care about the girls in his past anymore. In fact, it was pretty fun to tease him about it. "You're going to have to get me a *lot* more sangria if you expect that to work on me."

"I'll be right back with the punch bowl, then." Sebastian grinned down at Brett. "Don't go anywhere."

Brett leaned back again, closing her eyes. A fast-paced Beatles song came on the stereo. Jenny and Isaac had lit candles in the parlor, tiny tea lights lining the mantle and the piano, and light flickered romantically across the beautiful paintings on the wall. It was one of those great kinds of parties where everyone was drinking and being happy—dancing, laughing, and flirting—but no one was getting wasted or playing beer pong. It was like a grown-up soiree. Sophisticated. Not a game of I Never in sight.

Then the muffled but distinctive sound of "Living on a Prayer" burst her reverie. Sebastian's ringtone. Chuckling to herself, she sat up and fumbled through the pockets of his leather jacket, pulling out his phone. How did she shut this thing up? She pressed a few keys, managing to silence it. But as she did that, a screen popped up. It was his call log. And it was long. Apparently, Sebastian had been busy calling a lot of people.

Alexis. Leila. Hannah. Tricia. Someone named Sylvia. It didn't take too long for Brett to figure it out.

She got to her feet, which was difficult considering she felt like the floor had just fallen out from under them. The serenity she'd felt just moments ago had been completely shattered. How had she been so stupid, again? She'd finally let her guard down and believed in Sebastian. When was she going to learn? He was a *guy*, and guys didn't change. And they certainly couldn't be trusted.

Brett elbowed past the dance floor and threw open the hall closet, stuffed to the brim with winter coats. Where was her fucking coat?

"Hey, where are you going?" Sebastian appeared, holding two wineglasses full of sangria. He lowered his voice. "Do you want to make out in the coat closet, 'cause that would be hot."

"No," Brett snapped, finally finding her black mohair

peacoat and tearing it from the closet, sending the hanger clattering to the floor. "I'm going *home*."

A look of alarm crossed Sebastian's face as he noticed Brett holding his phone. She wanted to slap it into his hand, but he was holding two full wineglasses. She was forced to slip it into the pocket on the front of his shirt. Far less satisfying. "And I think you know why."

"Brett, come on. You're being stupid." Sebastian held out the glass of sangria to her.

"*What?*" She shrieked, her anger boiling over. She could feel people staring at her, but she didn't care. "You're calling me *stupid*? You must really think I am, don't you?"

"I'm sorry, I didn't mean it like that. You're not stupid—you're just acting stupid." Sebastian stepped aside and handed the full glasses to Alan St. Girard, who had just come through the front door after smoking a joint out on the porch. Sebastian put his hand on Brett's arm, but she shook it off. "You're totally overreacting. It's not what you think."

"Apparently, since I'm *stupid*, it doesn't matter what I think."

And before he could say anything else, Brett pushed her way through the cloud of marijuana smoke on the front porch and stomped off into the night.

WildernessMan Log: Heath vs. Wild

Day 55,999,999

Woke up in crippling pain. Legs cramping with cold. No raccoons. Thought we were all friends.

Temp: −666 degrees.

Food: PLEEEEEEEEEEASE.

Warmth: Need down comforter. Can't take. Much. More. Need. Heat.

Mood: So, so lonely. Where is everyone? What if Waverly disappeared while HF out in woods? What if HF was only survivor on face of earth?

Must . . . find . . . civilization.

A WAVERLY OWL ALWAYS KNOWS HOW TO MAKE A
GRAND ENTRANCE.

"Come on. Let's take a few more pictures." Isla grabbed Tinsley's wrist, almost tearing off her copper bangle bracelets, and tugged her toward a closed oak door. They were upstairs in the dean's house, in the coral-colored hallway. The music pulsed through the floor, and occasionally they'd hear the sounds of doors opening and closing as party-goers searched for a quiet place to make out.

"Oh, let's just hang out. Our project is perfect as is." Tinsley giggled. She was tipsy now, after drinking glass after glass of sangria on the dance floor with Isla. She hadn't kept track of how much she was drinking—it just felt too good to be moving her body on the tile-covered floor of the foyer. It felt like the old days again, back when all anyone could talk about was her and Brett and Callie. Except Brett was busy making out with her Italian stallion boyfriend, and Callie had clearly

lost her mind and was all cozy with Brandon Buchanan. *Again.*
What was going on with the world? Thank God for Isla. In her
black sequined Anna Sui miniskirt and a wifebeater, Isla looked
punk rock, the perfect foil to Tinsley's white silk Daughters
of the Revolution slip dress. They were a great pair. A perfect
match. Who needed a boyfriend when she had a ridiculously
cool best friend?

Isla flung open the door to a room at the end of the hallway
and lifted her empty glass into the air, giving an imaginary
toast. "Let's take pictures on my parents' bed, okay? In just our
underwear."

Tinsley blinked her eyes as she took in the enormous master
bedroom. The queen-size bed was covered in a sophisticated
gray-and-brown bed set, and, frankly, the last thing Tinsley
wanted to do was get naked on it. "Yeah, I'm not sure I want to
violate the dean's, uh, sacred sheets."

"Oh, boo." Isla set her wineglass down with a clank on a
book-covered nightstand and threw herself down on her parents' bed. Despite all the great things about her, Tinsley had
noticed that Isla had an incredible moody streak, and she sometimes had to placate her. "You're so boring."

Tinsley's stomach lurched. *Excuse me?* She was many things,
but boring was not one of them. "What if we take some shots in
the wine cellar?" she suggested. "Dancing around with bottles
of wine?"

Isla leaped up from the bed, her bare feet slapping against
the hardwood floor. "No, I have a way better idea." She latched
her hand onto Tinsley's wrist and dragged her back into

the hallway. Tinsley giggled. Isla's energy was infectious—exhausting, maybe, but infectious. "Look." She paused at the top of the staircase and pointed at the stained glass cupola over the foyer. The moonlight—from a full moon—lit up the gorgeous yellow and green art deco design of flowers.

"Maybe I'm drunk, but I don't get it." Tinsley watched the front door open down below—and held her breath for a second—before Lon Baruzza scooted inside, stomping the snow off his feet on the doormat. She hadn't realized she'd kept hoping Julian would show up until that moment.

But Isla was already off down the hallway. "Grab your camera. I'm going to head up the fire escape and get on the roof, and pose over that window." She winked over her shoulder at Tinsley. "And you're going to photograph me, from down below. I think the light is perfect—but we've got to do it before the moon goes behind a cloud."

"Wait, what are you talking about?" Tinsley instantly regretted all the sangria she'd downed—her brain felt sluggish, and her tongue was heavy in her mouth. "You're drunk—you can't climb up onto the roof."

"Don't be such a chicken." For a second, Isla's pale green eyes flashed with annoyance.

Almost immediately, Tinsley felt her hackles rise. She wasn't going to let anyone—even the dean's daughter—talk to her like that. "Seriously, Isla. It's not a good idea."

But then Isla laughingly blew her a kiss, and Tinsley relaxed. "Come on. Picture how amazing it'll be." Tinsley glanced up at the skylight and the way the moon lit it from above. Below, in the dimly lit foyer, bodies swayed on the dance floor, and the candles that lined the stairs looked like they were dancing, too. Everything seemed perfect and serene. "Just get the camera ready, please? It'll be such a great shot."

"Fine, fine. Give me a minute." Tinsley wobbled slightly, her red patent leather Alexander McQueen pumps feeling taller than she remembered. She sipped the last of her sangria before setting the empty glass on the floor. Resting her hand securely on the banister, she looked out over the foyer, trying to find the best spot to shoot Isla from. Finally, she settled on the very edge of the balcony, farthest from the stairs.

She stared up at the sky through the green-and-yellow window. There was a knot in the pit of her stomach. She took a deep breath through her nose, trying to calm her nerves. What were the odds that Isla could actually get on the roof? Maybe Tinsley should go check on her.

The music changed to something jazzy and mellow and soothing, and before she could move, Tinsley finally spotted a shadow above the window. She sucked in her breath. She could just make out the silhouette of Isla, whose body was leaning against the stained glass—and it was perfect. In awe, Tinsley clicked away. Isla was a genius. It was the perfect photograph, the epitome of contrast. A soft, shadowy body backlit against the hard-edged glass design. Isla spread her arms out, like wings. It looked like an angel had landed on the window.

A cold wind rushed up the stairs like a premonition, and Tinsley glanced down at the open door. Several of the candles on the stairs blew out. Two guys stepped through the doorway, but before Tinsley could register who they were, a terrible sound came from above. It took her a moment to realize what it was.

The cracking of glass.

Stunned, but still drunk, Tinsley's eyes flew back to the sky-light. A dozen snaking cracks appeared in the design. *Oh my God.* Tinsley opened her mouth to scream, but no sound came out. The people dancing on the black marble floor of the foyer hadn't noticed anything was wrong. Yet.

Once the glass started to break away from the skylight, everything moved in slow motion. Pieces of glass started to fall, making everyone on the dance floor look up. Someone shrieked. Benny and Alan St. Girard had been slow dancing, but they quickly jumped apart and joined the crush of bodies trying to crowd around the edges of the room. Everyone's eyes were pointed upward, people shielding their eyes with their hands to avoid the falling glass shards.

"There's someone up there!" Jenny's high-pitched voice called out. "It's a person!"

The sight of Isla's arms and legs outstretched, suspended in air above the foyer like some kind of magic trick, was strangely beautiful. Then Isla's body tumbled from its perch and, almost like it was floating, descended through the air. Camera still in hand, Tinsley reached out over the banister, as if there were something she could do to break her fall. She wished, crazily, that she could take a picture now of how gorgeous Isla looked in midair.

Tinsley held her breath as she waited for the moment of disaster. But suddenly someone rushed forward, stuck out his arms, and caught Isla, as if she were weightless. There was screaming as everyone crowded around them. Tinsley slowly made her way down the stairs, watching as people shook glass off their clothes and checked to make sure their friends were okay. Partygoers rushed in all directions, toward Isla and the guy who'd caught her, out the door, anywhere.

Tinsley stopped in the middle of the stairway. She hadn't been able to take her eyes off Isla's face. She looked shaken but unharmed. Finally, she tore her eyes away to see who was holding her friend. She blinked.

She suddenly wasn't so drunk anymore. The person holding Isla was awfully familiar.

**Owl**Net   Instant Message Inbox

SebastianValenti: Can you talk to me, please?

SebastianValenti: PLEASE?

[No response from BrettMesserschmidt.]

22

A WAVERLY OWL WELCOMES BACK AN OLD FRIEND

WITH OPEN ARMS.

"You know what we should do next weekend? Head up to Whiteface. Heath's parents said we could use their condo whenever we wanted this January." Brandon stroked his fingers against the side of Callie's cheek, and she closed her eyes. After the requisite socializing with their friends, she and Brandon had sneaked away. They'd found a cozy little den in the back of the house with an enormous fireplace. It wasn't lit, of course, but Brandon had stolen a couple of candles from the living room and placed them in the empty fireplace. He'd also brought a bottle of red wine, and now the two of them sat on an old couch that sagged in the middle, forcing them to snuggle in even more.

"The Ferros said you could use it?" Callie asked, shifting slightly, letting Brandon catch a glimpse down her plunging V-neck Rebecca Taylor dress. Underneath she wore her sexiest black lace-lined Cosabella camisole covered in rose petals and matching panties. It had been a long time since she had the urge to wear a matching set—without a boyfriend, it just seemed silly. "I thought Heath was banned after he left a condom there at his last party."

Brandon ran his fingers across Callie's collarbone. "Oh, *he's* not allowed to go there again." He chuckled. "But they love me. Last time I saw them, they gave me a key."

Callie laughed, reclining into the corner of the couch. "That would be fun. We could get a whole bunch of people to come up with us—Brett and Sebastian. Tinsley and Julian—well, not them, I guess, since that's kind of over." Callie smiled up at Brandon. Being with him was so . . . easy. He was sweet and kind, and constantly told her how gorgeous she was. She'd noticed the jealous eyes following them as they'd headed down the darkened hallway to the den. Making the female population of Waverly jealous was a nice little bonus.

Brandon leaned back on the couch. He picked up his wineglass and swirled it like an expert. "Yeah, he was a wreck when we played squash yesterday. Sounds like she was pretty harsh with him."

Callie frowned. "She didn't tell me much about it. She's always with *Isla*."

"It would be kind of fun if it was the two of us, alone, too. Right?" Brandon tickled Callie's bare leg and she giggled. It was so silly. Brandon had been here all along. He wasn't Easy Walsh, of course, but maybe that was a good thing. Easy was *dangerous*. Brandon was *nice*.

"Maybe," Callie answered automatically, even though the idea of the two of them alone sounded a little boring. She would work on him about the idea of having a ski party. They would be the hosts, like Isaac and Jenny tonight, and everyone would be completely jealous of what a gorgeous, elegant couple they made. She leaned forward to kiss him, and his mouth eagerly met hers. His hands slid behind her head, running through her hair. *How many people did the condo sleep?* Callie wondered, kissing him back absentmindedly as she planned out the guest list.

Her plans were interrupted by the sounds of shrieking coming from the front of the house. "What the hell is that?" Callie sprang to her feet, straightening her dress. She definitely didn't want to get caught by the new dean making out in his den.

Teague Williams, the senior basketball player, poked his head through the doorway of the den, reeking of weed. "Dude, all kinds of shit is happening."

"Is the dean back?" Callie asked, grabbing Brandon's hand and dragging him to his feet.

"Worse," Teague replied, his eyes glazed over with the stoner look. He stumbled over an ottoman as he made his way back out of the room. "The roof's caved in. Or something."

"Holy shit," Brandon whispered, still holding Callie's hand as he followed her through the crush of people in the living room. Everyone seemed to be clustered around the giant arched doorway that led to the foyer. Callie stood on her tiptoes, struggling to see over everyone's heads.

"She fell from the sky!" Verena Arneval kept repeating, a traumatized look on her pretty face. Lon had his arm around her shoulder and was rubbing her bare arm.

"Shit," Callie whispered, elbowing her way to the front of the crowd. "Come on," she snapped over her shoulder at Brandon as he struggled to keep up. Her feet crunched against the broken glass pieces that covered the floor as she stepped around Verena and Lon until she could see the center of the action. She gasped.

The scene in front of her was like something from a movie—shattered glass everywhere, girls with faces frozen in terror. It didn't seem real. Up above, where the skylight had been, there was a gaping, jagged hole looking out into the moonlit night. "Someone really did fall through the ceiling," Callie murmured. In the background, someone finally switched off the music, as if realizing the sound of Jason Mraz blaring through the sound system was somehow inappropriate.

Standing in the middle of it all was Isla Dresden, covered in broken glass, in the arms of a tall muscular guy. Her heart-shaped face was pale and shaken-looking, and her bare arms were covered in dark scratches. Callie felt badly for her. She hoped she wouldn't have any scars.

The guy finally set Isla carefully on her feet, and a shaky cheer rose up. Callie squinted at him curiously. His back was to her, but something about him was so familiar. That coat, a faded brown canvas thing. Something that looked standard issue or military. The wine had slowed Callie's brain, and she was struggling to put it together. The guy kept his arm around Isla protectively, even though she was safely on her own two feet.

Wait, that coat. She'd seen it, just once before. Could it really be . . .

Then, in one heart-pounding moment, she realized:

It was Easy.

Callie sucked in her breath, feeling like she'd fallen through the ceiling herself. What the *hell* was Easy doing back at Waverly? In his military school coat that he'd worn that terrible day, on top of the Empire State Building. When Callie handed him back the promise ring he'd given her. How did he get here? And why?

And why the fuck did he still have his arm around the dean's daughter?

A queasy, shaky, slightly nauseated feeling started in the pit of her stomach and somehow managed to creep up her throat and down her arms until she felt her whole body start to quake.

As if he could feel her stare, Easy looked up. His blue eyes met Callie's across the room, and a jolt of lightning shot through her. She couldn't think of a single thing to do besides mouth the word *Hi*.

He mouthed it back to her. His arm was still supporting Isla, damsel in distress, but Callie watched Easy's eyes turn to Brandon, who was still holding Callie's hand. Flustered, Callie let his hand drop.

"You okay?" Brandon looked back and forth from Callie to the glass-strewn scene in front of them. The second he saw Easy Walsh, he knew it was trouble. And Callie's face proved he was right. "Come on. We should get out of here."

"Huh?" Callie stared at him as if she'd never seen him before. "I'm . . . okay." She touched her forehead with her fingertips.

"What's he doing here?" Brandon asked, a lump in his throat. Of all the parties in all the world, why the hell did Easy Walsh have to wander into this one?

"And is that . . . Heath?" Brandon stared at the bedraggled, bearded figure next to Easy, chugging a half-empty bottle of red wine like some kind of alcoholic who'd fallen off the wagon.

His dirty blond hair looked tangled and filthy from his stay in the woods. His hunter green fleece was covered with crushed leaves, and his cheeks were wind-burned and stubbly.

Callie finally met Brandon's gaze. Now that Easy was back, nothing was the same. She'd forgotten all about Brandon the second Easy stepped through the doorway. It was like history repeating itself. "I . . ." Callie stammered.

Brandon grabbed Callie's hand and tugged her gently down the back hall toward the kitchen, away from the foyer. "Let's get out of here. I'll walk you home."

Callie glanced over her shoulder. She didn't want Easy to see her leaving with Brandon, but he was no longer looking at her. He was pulling a piece of glass out of Isla's hair.

Callie blinked, then followed Brandon out the door.

Jenny finally managed to push through the crowd to reach Isla and Easy, shards of glass glittering in her dark hair. She'd grabbed a broom from the hall closet, as if there were some way for her to sweep the whole mess under the rug. "It's okay, everyone. Isla's fine. Just, you know, stay calm."

She spun around the foyer. From the wreckage, it was impossible to believe Isla could actually be all right. But Isaac had checked her for broken bones, and Easy was still propping her up. Easy. Jenny's stomach was shaking—she'd been in the foyer, on her way into the dining room, when Isla crashed through the window. And Easy had just reached out and plucked her from the air, like some kind of superhero. It was insane. Jenny had caught his eye as he stood there in a blur of shattered glass and screaming girls. When he smiled at her with those familiar deep blue eyes, Jenny's heart almost stopped. He was stronger now from doing drills at military school, and more clean-cut. He even looked like a superhero.

"You know . . ." Isaac looked at Jenny anxiously. "I think we should get everyone out of here as quickly as possible."

"Of course," Jenny replied, staring at the floor. It was going to be a disaster to clean up, and to try and explain to the dean what happened. She might be able to keep the party a secret, but there was no concealing property damage. She was in deep, deep shit. "We've got a lot of cleaning up to do."

Isaac smiled when Jenny said "we." "I didn't mean that—just that I think the house has some kind of . . ." Before he could finish, through the open front door, the flashing lights of a campus security patrol car were visible as it pulled up the driveway.

"Silent alarm," he finished.

"RUN!" Heath Ferro started grabbing the closest girls and herding them toward the back of the house. "Everyone head to the closest emergency exit!"

"Everyone stay where you are!" the squat security officer shouted as he stepped out of his car and thundered up the front steps. "Don't move!"

Too late. The entire party quickly raced toward the kitchen exit or through the sliding glass doors in the living room. Jenny spotted a couple of guys throwing open a window in the dining room and jumping out into the bushes.

Isaac pushed Jenny toward the kitchen, his hands warm against the small of her back. Sage Francis and a bunch of others funneled out the side door and rushed across the snowy yard back to the dorms, leaving a massive trail of footprints in their wake. The bare arms of the girls shone in the moonlight, and they ran faster to stay warm. "But I can't leave you here to deal with this . . ." Jenny protested, a cold gust of wind sweeping into the kitchen. Sangria-encrusted wineglasses were scattered around the kitchen counters, and empty wine bottles were still stacked in the sink.

"Go," Isaac insisted, handing Jenny her red peacoat, which she'd left hanging next to the kitchen door. "I'll think of something."

Still, Jenny paused in the doorway, reluctant to leave. She didn't want Isaac to get in trouble, but she also didn't want the dean to walk into his ruined house and find her there, either. The combination of sangria and adrenaline running through her veins made it hard to think straight. And just thinking about the disaster in the foyer made it feel like she had a block of ice sitting in her stomach. How the hell were they going to get out of that one?

Isaac finally planted his hands on Jenny's shoulders and shoved her, gently but firmly, toward the door. He winked at her, even though his face looked anxious. "I think my first Waverly party qualifies as a success."

Jenny tried to laugh as more people brushed by them, pushing them closer together. Isaac was so close, she could smell his toothpaste. He could probably count the freckles on her face. "Are you sure?" Despite the arrival of the security guards, she didn't want to leave.

"I had a lot of fun tonight. With you." Isaac reached up to brush a loose curl off her cheek, and Jenny's heart beat faster.

"I had fun, too," she said softly, staring at her shoes. She was frustrated that they didn't have more time for goodbyes. The party had been so perfect, it was a shame it had to end like this. "I was kind of looking forward to cleaning up with you."

"Next time." Isaac grinned. Someone stumbled on his way out the door, elbowing Jenny in the back and pressing her right into Isaac. His hands flew to her waist to steady her.

Before she could register exactly what was happening, Isaac was bending down toward her. His lips touched softly against hers, and she felt a million butterflies fluttering in her stomach. Everything—the partygoers streaming out the door, the cold rush of air as it opened and closed, the smell of spilled sangria— faded into the background. Nothing mattered but the way his lips felt against hers, and the minty taste of his mouth.

Finally, Isaac pulled away. Jenny blinked as she returned to reality. It took her a second to realize she was still in the kitchen. A couple of stragglers stared at them as they scuttled out the door. "Okay, enough distracting me already," Isaac said, touching Jenny's elbow lightly. "You've got to get out of here."

"Are you sure?" Jenny asked, biting her lip. Her lips felt like they were on fire.

"Positive." He pushed her out the door as Rifat Jones and Lon Baruzza dashed out. Rifat shot Jenny a thumbs-up that Isaac pretended to ignore. Jenny's legs managed to carry her down the short wooden staircase, but she still felt like she was floating. She glanced over her shoulder at Isaac. He was still standing in the doorway, watching her leave. "You're too cute to get into trouble," he called after her.

If only that were true.

OwlNet

From: SebastianValenti@waverly.edu
To: BrettMesserschmidt@waverly.edu
Date: Saturday, January 8, 8:19 P.M.
Subject: You

CALL ME! I'm not explaining this over e-mail.

A WAVERLY OWL ALWAYS TAKES CREDIT FOR HER

OWN IDEAS.

Tinsley's legs felt like jelly as she made her way down to Isla and Easy. She'd been too stunned to move at first, and she was pretty sure she was still in shock. She made it halfway down the stairs before she found her legs wouldn't take her any farther. Holding on to the banister, she watched as the security guards raced into the house, chasing the last of the frantic students as they escaped out the back doors and windows. Isla, Easy Walsh, and Isaac were the only others who remained.

When she felt like she could breathe again, she finally made her way downstairs, wobbling on her high heels. Isla was now standing in the middle of the glass-covered foyer, picking pieces of glass out of her messy dark hair. Isaac appeared from the kitchen, carrying a glass of water and handed it to her. The guy next to her—definitely, undeniably Easy Walsh—was still looking at her, concerned.

"Are you okay, sweetie?" Tinsley asked, glass crunching under her shoes, as she came up and put her hand on Isla's shoulder. Gently. Her skin was marked with dozens of red scratches, most of which looked like surface cuts. Someone had slid a pair of men's shoes onto Isla's bare feet before setting her down on the glass-covered floor. She had a dazed look on her face, and she was still leaning against Easy's tall, lean body. "We need to take you to the health center. Have them check you out."

Isla blinked her pale green eyes at Tinsley and gave a shaky laugh. Her dark, curly hair was wild and tangled, although the look actually suited her. "I'm fine, thanks to this handsome stranger."

Tinsley looked up at Easy, who was standing there in a pair of battered hiking shoes and an ugly brown coat. His beautiful unruly hair had been completely shorn off at military school, making him look older and harder, but also highlighting his perfect bone structure. His skin was tanned, and his lean body was tighter, stronger looking. Tinsley imagined him doing hundreds of pushups a day and running through obstacle courses in the mud. He looked more serious than Tinsley remembered. But maybe that was because he'd just saved someone's life.

"Um, I'm glad you walked through this door at the most perfect time in the world and all, but . . . what the *hell* are you doing here?" Tinsley stared at him, awestruck.

"Long story." Easy chuckled softly. His gentle Kentucky accent was more pronounced than before. She'd heard his military school was down south somewhere, like the backwoods of

West Virginia. "Basically, I ran away. I really just wanted to see Credo again."

Tinsley almost felt like crying. She leaned forward and gave him a quick peck on the cheek. "Thank God you did. You saved Isla's life." It seemed absolutely crazy that Easy could show up at Waverly to check on his *horse* and arrive on exactly the right night, at exactly the right time.

"I don't know about that." An embarrassed grin broke out on his face. "I was on my way to the stables when I ran into Heath in the woods." He shrugged casually, as if it was no big deal. "He never could miss a party."

Isla smiled up at Easy through her long, thick eyelashes. "Really, it must have been fate that you got here when you did," she said, touching his arm. "Otherwise, I'd have . . ." She shivered. Theatrically. Isla had just managed to escape breaking her neck, and here she was flirting with a hot guy. Already. Not bad.

"You guys should probably head out." Isaac appeared, a huge push broom in his hand as he swept up the shards of glass that dotted the foyer. "The security guards are chasing after the others, so you could probably sneak out of here without anyone noticing."

Tinsley opened her mouth to agree, but before she could, the front door flew open once more. Dean Dresden appeared in the doorway, his ashen-faced wife at his side. They both had on long black coats, scarves thrown hastily around their necks.

"Isla, security said there was an accident. Are you hurt?" The dean stepped forward as Mrs. Dresden threw her arms around Isla, who immediately burst into tears. Tinsley blinked her eyes. From femme fatale to weeping child in three seconds? Even *she* wasn't that good.

"I'm fine, Daddy." She pulled away from her mother, wiping at her tears with her wrist, and threw herself into her father's arms. Isla hadn't been traumatized a minute ago, when she was hitting on Easy Walsh. But Tinsley couldn't blame her for putting on the teary-eyed act—Dean Dresden looked furious. She hoped he'd be lenient with Isla, at least, given what she'd just gone through. She hadn't meant to do anything wrong—she just had pretty terrible judgment.

"She's all right, sir," one of the security guards spoke up. The shoulders of his dark maroon jacket were dusted in snow. "She managed to land in someone's arms, and it looks like she just has some cuts and bruises. You probably want to get her checked out at the health center."

"Oh, Isla, I'm just glad you're safe." The dean's voice turned stern as he stepped away from his daughter. In his dark suit and black overcoat, he looked dapper but intimidating. "But I don't enjoy being called away from an important evening with my new faculty to come home to . . . this." He swept his arm out over the shattered glass of the foyer. Shards of metal littered the area, and pieces of splintered wood hung down from the gaping hole in the ceiling. "This disaster area. Tell me, how on *earth* did this happen?" Tinsley's mouth twisted as she waited for the ax to fall on her friend. Clearly, Isla was not going to escape punishment. It wasn't fair, really. The whole thing was an accident.

Tinsley stepped forward, her heels crunching against the glass. She knew it was never smart for an outsider to interfere with parental disciplining, but she couldn't just stand by and watch her friend get reamed out.

But Isla spoke first. "Daddy, I'm so sorry. I didn't want to get up on the roof." Her sea-green eyes teared up again, the tears spilling out over her cheeks. "But Tinsley kept insisting what a great shot it would make. It was all her idea."

Tinsley's jaw dropped. What? *She'd* told *Isla* it was a terrible idea. Tinsley's eyes flashed up to meet Easy's. He looked skeptical about Isla's story. If a perfect *stranger* could tell it was a lie, couldn't her parents?

Isla started to sob openly. "I was so . . . scared."

"Oh, baby." Mrs. Dresden threw her arms around Isla, shooting daggers toward Tinsley.

Tinsley's mouth felt dry as the dean's eyes turned to her. Was there any way he'd take her own word . . . over his own daughter's? Her heart sunk as she realized how unlikely that was. He'd probably seen Tinsley's file, in fact, and knew that she'd already been kicked out of Waverly once. Maybe even Isla knew.

"Tinsley, is this true?" The dean's voice was cold.

Tinsley glanced at Isla. She didn't know what she expected—a wink, a secret nod, anything. But instead, Isla's eyes were icy and distant.

Suddenly it all made sense. Isla said she loved hanging with the *most interesting* kids. Of course. Isla probably did the same thing at every school—find out who the kids with the worst records were, befriend them, and then, when things fell apart, lay the blame accordingly. It was the perfect alibi.

That bitch. She'd underestimated Isla, clearly. Tinsley definitely *had* met her match. But not in a good way.

"Dean Dresden—" she began, searching for the words to defend herself.

But the dean cut her off. "Miss Carmichael. Be in my office Monday morning. Eight o'clock sharp. We'll discuss this then." The dean's lips pressed together in a straight line.

"Dad, listen." Isaac spoke up, placing his hand on his father's forearm. "I don't think it was Tinsley's fault."

"This doesn't concern you," Dean Dresden replied sharply.

Tinsley felt her own eyes start to sting, but she'd be damned if she let that bitch make her cry. She bit her lip and turned to the coat closet off the entryway. Coats were scattered everywhere. She flicked aside a stack of black peacoats, searching for her gray Michael Kors. She'd never wanted to disappear so badly in her life.

"And Isaac," she overheard the dean saying, "you are going to make me a list of every single person who was at the party tonight."

"Dad, I can't do that. . . ."

Tinsley finally grabbed her coat and peeked into the hallway just in time to see the dean hold out a hand to Easy Walsh, who had been standing there awkwardly the entire time. "Now, young man, I'm dying to know to whom I owe my daughter's life."

Some people have all the luck.

OwlNet

AlanStGirard: Sorry our dance got interrupted. Those security dudes are so rude!

BennyCunningham: S'all right—not like U were getting anywhere, anyway!

AlanStGirard: Man, that shit was fucked up. Good thing Isla's okay.

BennyCunningham: That was insane! Was that really Easy?

AlanStGirard: Hells yeah it was. His bag is already back in the room. Good thing they never gave me a new roomie.

BennyCunningham: How'd he escape military school?

AlanStGirard: Sorry, sugar. My lips are sealed. Unless, of course, you're offering to unseal them.

OwlNet   Instant Message Inbox

RyanReynolds: Quick—guess what bra size the dean's wife is.

BrandonBuchanan: What? Dude, you are fucking sick. That's all
                      you can think about?

RyanReynolds: Yes. 34D. I even took a pair of panties to go
                      with!

BrandonBuchanan: Didn't U hear that Heath is back? U don't have
                      to be the resident perv anymore.

Owl Net

CelineColista: I saw that fat security guy look straight at me—the 'rents will kill me if I get in trouble!

AlisonQuentin: Don't worry. They don't know who U are. Or who anyone else was. We're safe.

CelineColista: Good. Man, I need to sober up!

AlisonQuentin: How hot did Easy look? Military school does a body goooood.

CelineColista: Right? Did U see the look on Cal's face? Looks like Brandon is screwed—again!

AlisonQuentin: I'll take Callie's sloppy seconds anytime.

A WAVERLY OWL MAKES AN EFFORT TO BOND WITH
HER DORMMATES.

Jenny eased down the creaky staircase of Dumbarton Hall later that night. Even in the safety of her favorite slippers, she still felt like there was a giant lead ball sitting in her stomach. They'd destroyed the new dean's house and practically killed his daughter. Shit was going to hit the fan.

She poked her head into the common room. Despite the fact that it was almost lights out, Angelica Pardee, their dorm mistress, had already turned in and told them not to stay up too late. She clearly hadn't heard about the epic party at the dean's house yet, otherwise she would undoubtedly have made sure all her charges were sequestered in their rooms.

Everyone looked up when Jenny entered the room. "Legendary party, Jenny!" Benny Cunningham, in a pair of gray silk pajamas, lounged with her legs thrown over an armchair. She threw a piece of buttery popcorn in Jenny's direction. "I particularly liked the surprise ending."

Jenny blushed and headed over to the blue velvet sofa, sitting down beside Brett. "I'm glad I missed it," Brett said quietly. She'd left right after her Sebastian fallout and was glad she'd avoided the chaos. But she was also secretly happy that everybody came home early. It had been lonely, sitting here by herself in the common room, driving herself crazy thinking about where Sebastian was and whom he was with.

"Yeah, I saw you screaming at Sebastian. What was *that* all about?" Benny leaned forward, her eyes greedy for gossip.

Jenny could tell Brett didn't want to talk about it, so she spoke up. "I thought everything was going well until the whole crashing-through-the-skylight thing." She tried to make her voice sound light, but she was really worried. She kept thinking about Isaac, hoping he wasn't going to get in too much trouble. She felt terrible about leaving him alone to face the music.

Celine Colista, wearing a skimpy Only Hearts nightie, tucked her legs up under her and wrapped a fleece Waverly Owls blanket around her shoulders. She sipped from a bottle of spiked Gatorade. "Who cares? The party will go down in history—and all the better, since no one got busted."

Benny giggled drunkenly. "I can't believe we all got out before those security guards could catch anyone."

"I can't believe she actually fell through the roof!" Alison replied, stumbling slightly across the room before collapsing into an empty armchair. Jenny had seen her down three glasses of sangria, and with her tiny frame, that had to have made an impact. Lon Baruzza, who'd been flirting with her all night, was probably extra pissed that the party got broken up.

"*Hello!*" Benny wrapped a pink cashmere blanket tighter around her. "What about Easy Walsh, appearing out of nowhere? Wasn't *that* incredible?"

"Why do you think he came back?" Brett asked, staring right at Callie.

Immediately, Callie felt everyone's eyes on her. She hadn't been able to stop thinking about Easy since she saw him, wondering the same exact thing. Why had he come back? Was it . . . for her?

"So, I don't get it, Cal. Are you and Brandon together, or what?" Benny asked, pulling her light brown hair into a ponytail.

Callie glared at Benny. She and Brandon had shared an awkward goodbye as they ran from the security guards. Although they didn't talk about it, she was pretty sure he was thinking about Easy being back, too. She had no idea what was going to happen tomorrow. Was it possible that Easy was back for good? Now that she had seen him again, the idea of him leaving before she could talk to him made her sick to her stomach. Was he thinking about her right now? Where was he sleeping? Could he really tell that Brandon had been holding her hand? "I don't know," she said finally, feigning a yawn to avoid further questioning.

"How about Heath?" Brett jumped in, seeing the distress on Callie's face. Callie shot her a grateful look. "I don't think I've ever seen him looking dirtier."

"I wondered how long he'd be able to last in the woods."
Jenny giggled. The other girls weren't worried about getting in
trouble, so maybe she shouldn't be, either. Maybe things would
work out. "Without female contact."

"I've totally missed him," Benny admitted. "It's kind of nice
to have someone around to leer at you."

There was a pounding on the front door of Dumbarton, and
Jenny jumped. "Who is that?" she hissed.

"Don't be such a chicken," Benny replied crankily, standing up and stepping into her Mephisto clogs. "It's not security. They'd just come in." She clomped over to the door and
threw it open. A rush of cold air burst into the foyer, along with
an almost blue Sage Francis and Verena Arneval, still wearing
their high heels and party dresses.

"Holy fuck, it's cold out." Sage stumbled through the door,
giggling and rubbing her bare arms. "Thanks for letting us in."

"Our ID cards were in our coat pockets," Verena explained,
lunging for the throw blanket on the back of the common-
room couch.

"Wait, what?" Brett's eyes widened. "You guys left your
coats there? With your IDs in them?"

"But if they have our IDs . . ." Verena trailed off.

"They know who we are," Benny finished the sentence,
throwing herself into an armchair. "Fuck! I didn't even think of
that. A bunch of us ran into Yvonne Stidder on the way home
and she opened the front door. I didn't even notice I was card-
less."

Jenny met Brett's eyes. Brett, as junior class prefect, probably had a good idea what kind of punishments would result from an illegal, alcohol-fueled party that ended with someone falling through the roof.

"We're totally fucked," Sage wailed, grabbing a random fleece from the coatrack in the living room that the girls used as a lost and found. She wrapped it around her shoulders. "I can't believe I thought we were in the clear."

The sound of another knock at the door startled the room. Everyone watched, terrified this time, as Sage cautiously pushed open the door. Instead of an angry security guard, Heath Ferro whirled in, pausing to throw his arms around Sage and give her a long, wet kiss on her cheek. "Did I smell popcorn, ladies?"

"Heath, get out of here," Callie snapped, pushing him away as he tried to hug her. His chin was covered with a blondish stubble, and his cheeks were ruddy and tanned. The scruffy look actually suited him, but after all the rumors about him eating poor, defenseless squirrels, Callie was kind of grossed out.

"I can't help it. I've been deprived of female contact for too long." His green eyes eagerly scanned the room, taking in the pajama-clad girls sprawled on the sofas and chairs. He threw himself down on a couch between Brett and Jenny. "This is like heaven for me."

"Seriously, we're in enough trouble already." Brett shoved Heath's arm off her. He smelled like a combination of Pine-Sol and BO. "Leave."

"Trouble?" Heath asked, snatching a lock of Jenny's hair and holding it under his nose. His eyes rolled back into his

head as if he were about to faint with pleasure. Jenny quickly
pulled her hair out of his hand and inched away from him.

"Oh shit," Brett exclaimed, getting to her feet as a terrible thought crossed her mind. Although she hadn't been stupid enough to leave her ID card behind, she *had* been stupid
enough to leave the monogrammed silk scarf her grandmother
had given her for her birthday last year. How many Waverly
Owls shared her same initials? It would take the dean about five
minutes to figure out who it belonged to.

At that exact moment, like a sign from above, everyone's
phones buzzed. Except Jenny's. She stared at her mysteriously
silent Treo as everyone else flicked open their phones.

"An e-mail from the dean," Brett confirmed, running her
hand through her hair.

"Please tell me he says we're all under house arrest and have
to stay exactly where we are for the rest of Jan Plan," Heath
said, pressing his hands together in prayer at the thought of
being locked in the Dumbarton common room with the pret-
tiest girls in school.

"Let me see." Jenny peered over Heath's shoulder to read
the e-mail on Brett's phone. It was addressed to a long list of
people—everyone who had been at the party.

Brett continued to read aloud. "From the coats, ID cards"—
Sage Francis groaned—"and cell phones left behind, along
with several photographs taken by security as students fled the
scene, we've managed to compile a list of those who attended
the party," Brett read. "If you are receiving this e-mail, you are
officially on academic probation. Everyone must report to my

office at eight o'clock sharp on Monday morning to receive your punishment. In the meantime, you may pick up your abandoned belongings in the Stansfield Hall lobby."

"Sincerely, your new dean," Benny added in a snide voice. "I guess he's no James Bond, after all."

"Isn't it ironic that I'm not in trouble for once?" Heath asked, sinking back into the couch with a satisfied grin on his face. "Since I'm, like, the king of Waverly parties."

"You were there, remember?" Sage snapped, pushing her silky blond hair off her forehead.

"Yeah, but only at the end. And I was part of the rescue party, so it doesn't count." Heath blew Sage a kiss.

"*Easy* was the knight in shining armor who rescued Isla, not you." Benny pointed out, staring at her cell phone in disgust.

"Walsh was only there because I brought him, so Isla's indebted to me, too." Heath practically licked his lips. "So he better not think he's getting her without a fight."

"How come your name's not on this list, Jenny?" Callie pointed out, her hazel eyes scowling. Why did Heath even think Easy wanted Isla to begin with? Did he know something? "*You're* the one who threw the party!"

"Are you sure I'm not on it?" Jenny asked meekly, staring at the list of names. "I mean, I don't know why I wouldn't have gotten the e-mail, too." Her palms felt clammy all of a sudden as she felt everyone's eyes on her. The stupid party had been her idea in the first place—and now she was the only one not in trouble? That didn't make any sense. Although her coat had been easy to retrieve, she was pretty sure she'd left, on the kitchen counter, the tiny Moleskine sketchbook she kept on her at all times in case she saw something she wanted to draw. And written in her very readable calligraphy on the inside front cover was the name Jenny Humphrey. The dean had to have found it.

Unless Isaac did first.

"I don't see Isaac or Isla's names on here, either," Benny pointed out, her porcelain skin reddening with indignation. Even though five minutes ago she'd been raving about how legendary the party was, she glared at Jenny as if she'd dragged her there by her thumbs. "And it was their freaking house!"

Jenny sank back into the sofa, listening to everyone bicker. But even worse than her friends' icy glares was the sinking suspicion that Isaac had done this to protect her. And that he thought this was what she wanted. After all, she'd already gotten special treatment on more than one occasion because of him. The dean had given her permission to do her art project solo because of his son's interference, and she didn't get busted for being out after curfew because she'd been with him.

Now, it seemed, she was being spared from punishment when *she* was the one who'd suggested the illicit party in the first place.

Jenny felt the angry stares, and her face grew hot. For the first time in her life, she wished she were in trouble.

OwlNet   Instant Message Inbox

AlanStGirard: Know what I said about that party rocking? I take it back.

BennyCunningham: This sucks. If the dean wants to make a good first impression, he's doing a shitty job.

AlanStGirard: Probation sucks, too. I should know. It's my third time.

BennyCunningham: How embarrassing is that for me? I'm on DC!

AlanStGirard: Wanna come over and brainstorm a way to get out of this?

BennyCunningham: No thanks.

OwlNet   Email Inbox

From: IslaDresden@waverly.edu
To: TinsleyCarmichael@waverly.edu
Date: Saturday, January 8, 10:48 P.M.
Subject: C'est la vie, sister

Sorry, babe, but you know you would've done the same thing to me.

Xx

A WAVERLY OWL DOES NOT LEAVE HER DORM
ROOM AFTER LIGHTS OUT WITHOUT A VERY
GOOD REASON.

It was after midnight, and Callie had counted the faded glow-in-the dark stars stuck to the ceiling above her bed a billion times. But they wouldn't help her fall asleep. Not tonight. Not when Easy was somewhere on campus. Her whole body was wired, as if she'd chugged twelve lattes, and her mind kept replaying the scene at the end of the party. Easy, standing there in the middle of all the chaos, staring straight at Callie: she should have talked to him. Asked him what the hell he was doing back at Waverly. Instead, she stood there like an idiot, holding Brandon's hand and mouthing *Hi* like she was some kind of parrot.

Across the room, Jenny, who usually slept like a baby, turned for the thousandth time in her bed. The springs squeaking beneath her were like fingernails on a chalkboard. Callie couldn't lie in bed listening to that any longer. She threw off her thick down comforter and jumped to her feet.

Jenny sat up in bed, her hair a tangled mess around her head. "What are you doing?" she asked sleepily. She stared at Callie as she stepped out of her cashmere pajama pants and grabbed the pair of dark Stella McCartney skinny jeans slung over her desk chair.

"I can't sleep." Callie tugged her navy blue Ralph Lauren cable-knit sweater from the closet and threw it on over her pink camisole. She pulled on a pair of thick wool socks and grabbed her red Marc by Marc Jacobs duck boots. "I've got to get some air."

Jenny sat up. "But Pardee . . . she'll hear you leave."

"I'll be quiet." Callie grabbed a black fleece she never wore from the back of her closet—she might as well try to blend in with the night. "Look, I just have to walk around a little. Clear my head."

"You're going to look for Easy, aren't you?" Jenny asked softly, pulling her quilt up around her.

Callie blinked. Who was she kidding? She wasn't going for a walk to clear her head. She'd been waiting for the sound of rocks at her window, the sign that Easy was waiting for her below. If he'd wanted to see her, he would have known where to find her. But maybe he was too proud to. "I guess. Wish me luck." Callie zipped the fleece up to her chin. She had to talk to him. The thought of Easy was like an itch in her brain, and she couldn't imagine doing anything else until she saw him. She was hoping that somehow, wherever he was, Easy wasn't able to sleep, either.

"Bring your cell," Jenny said, her brown eyes sympathetic. "You can text me when you need to get back in." Callie flashed her a grateful grin before slipping out the door.

She slunk down the quiet hallways, holding her breath as she passed Pardee's door. She silently made it out the front of Dumbarton and slid her socked feet into her boots out on the porch. The night was dark and crisp, and Callie's breath froze the second it left her mouth. Her feet crunched down the salted pathways. A billion stars were visible in the inky black sky. She knew exactly where she was going.

By the time the dark red stables at the edge of campus came into view, Callie's hands were nearly frozen. She'd forgotten her gloves. The smell of horses hit her forcefully, sending all her memories of Easy rushing back. She hadn't been back here since he'd been expelled because it would have been too painful. It felt like just yesterday that they'd been lying in the clean hay, kissing. He *had* to be here.

Callie glanced around for Groundskeeper Ben's telltale flashlight, but the only movement she saw was a fat owl swooping down from the bare branches of an oak tree. She shivered and stepped toward the stable door, pushing it open with her shoulder.

A couple of horses shuffled and whinnied; then there was silence. The stables were pitch black except for the beam of moonlight streaming through the small window over the tack room. The building was empty save for the horses.

Tears of frustration filled Callie's eyes. She didn't know why she'd been so certain that Easy would be here. It was stupid, but she always felt like she had some kind of Easy-radar. She could tell the moment he entered the dining hall or when he stepped out of a crowded party for a cigarette. It made her feel like they'd had some sort of mystical connection.

Apparently, any connection had been severed the moment she dumped him.

Callie wandered down the aisle in the center of the stables, not ready to head back to her room. Her eyes had adjusted to the dim light and she stepped on a piece of what she hoped was mud. She looked up in surprise when she noticed she was in front of Credo's stall. Easy's horse had remained at Waverly even after his expulsion because of some complication with bringing her back to Kentucky. Credo's huge brown eyes were watching Callie closely, and she reached out a bare hand to touch the horse's soft forehead.

"What are you doing here?"

Callie shrieked. Standing in the shadows of Credo's stall was Easy Walsh.

"It's okay," Easy said in a calming voice to Credo, running his hand gently along the horse's back. Easy shot her a look. "Don't you know not to scream in front of a horse?"

"Sorry," Callie apologized, smoothing down her hair nervously. Her own heart was beating out of control. "You scared the shit out of me."

"I thought maybe it was Ben." Easy shrugged as he stepped forward and leaned his elbows on top of the wooden gate to Credo's stall. He was still wearing the ugly military school coat he'd had on at the party, but it somehow made him look even more rugged and sexy. In the moonlight, his tanned skin glowed and his blue eyes gleamed bright. Callie wished he weren't on the other side of the wooden door. "I didn't want to get kicked out—again."

Callie laughed awkwardly. The sound echoed through the lofty stables. She inched closer to the gate. "How did you get here, Easy?" And *why*, she wanted to ask but couldn't. Credo couldn't be the only thing that had brought him back.

Easy yawned as he ran a hand over his short dark hair. "I bribed the car service that was supposed to take me back to military school. They let me off at the bus station instead."

Callie felt his eyes boring into her. She knew he'd seen her at the party. He must have noticed Brandon holding her hand. Did he care? She bit her chapped lip. "Well, I'm glad you're here, even though your parents are probably flipping out."

That brought a crooked grin to Easy's face, and Callie felt her knees weaken. "They were sending me back to school early, so I should have another day or two before they notice I'm gone."

"But what are you going to *do*?" Callie asked urgently. She leaned forward on the gate, her hand accidentally brushing against Easy's knuckles. She jumped back quickly. "I mean, you can't hide out in the stables forever." Of course he couldn't. But the thought of Easy leaving again . . . it was a thought she didn't even want to entertain.

"I don't have to." Easy stepped away from the gate and grabbed a horse brush hanging at the side of the stall. He started to brush down Credo, who tossed her head in approval. "Dresden told me since I kind of saved Isla, he was going to go ahead and reinstate me. He'll make it official tomorrow." He said the words casually, as if the dean revoking expulsion was something that happened every day.

"*What?*" Callie's jaw dropped almost to her feet. Easy was back . . . for good? "Oh my God. Easy, that's incredible." She felt faint. What would it mean to have Easy back? Would everything be like it was before? Just hearing him say the name *Isla* felt like angry pricks all over her skin. She hoped he wouldn't feel grateful to the dean's daughter for inadvertently helping him back into Waverly.

Easy took a deep breath and pushed the gate open. He stepped out into the aisle, hay crunching beneath his sneakers. He gave her a long look that made her forget about whatever the hell she'd stepped in tonight. "You look good," he said gruffly.

"You, too." Callie felt a lump in her throat. She took a step toward him, and reached her hand up to run across his head. Her body shook a little when she touched him. "Even with short hair."

Easy stared down at her. Callie felt her eyes lock on to his and that familiar gravitational pull take over. Easy's blue eyes, up close, looked confused. But he wasn't exactly pushing her away. Their lips inched closer and closer together until finally, after what felt like eternity, they met. Callie closed her eyes and pressed her body against Easy's. Every inch of her felt alive. She felt his hands clutch her tangled hair, pulling her even closer. Their mouths moved frantically against each other. It had been so long since they kissed—really kissed—that Callie felt a familiar stirring in the pit of her stomach.

"Wait. No." Easy backed up abruptly.

"What?" Callie tried to catch her breath. She touched Easy's arm but he shook her hand off gently. "What's wrong?"

He smiled sadly as he rubbed his chin with his hand. "Aren't you going to tell me what's going on with you and Buchanan?"

Callie stood up straighter. She reached for her hair, trying to smooth out the parts Easy had ruffled. "What about Brandon?" she asked petulantly.

"I saw you guys holding hands." Easy leaned back against Credo's stall, and his horse poked her head over and nuzzled his shoulder. Easy turned and made a soft cooing noise into the animal's ear. Callie stared at the horse jealously. She wanted Easy to be whispering in *her* ear.

Callie took a deep breath. She drew a half circle in the dusty floor with the toe of her boot. "I don't really know what's going on."

Easy stroked the horse's velvety nose with his hand. "Besides, I seem to remember you telling me you couldn't be with me anymore. That it was over. On top of the Empire State Building, remember?"

Callie felt as if she'd been punched in the lungs. Yes, she had said that. But things had been so different then. It was after she hadn't seen Easy in weeks, or even *talked* to him. Not a single e-mail or text. She barely knew he was alive. And she'd lost the promise ring he'd given her. She just hadn't been herself.

"I know. But I don't think it is." She took a deep breath and stared across the aisle at Easy. Her stomach was doing somersaults. "Do you?"

Easy sighed heavily, and turned away from her. "I guess we'll have to wait and see."

A WAVERLY OWL ALWAYS GIVES HER BOYFRIEND A
CHANCE TO EXPLAIN BEFORE SHE FLIPS OUT.

Brett sat in the reading area on the first floor of Sawyer Library on Sunday morning, her back to the enormous plate glass windows that looked out over the quad. Mrs. Birdsall, the icy old librarian, had gone upstairs, probably to try and catch some kids making out in the stacks, and Brett took the opportunity to pull a Nature Valley bar from her bag and take a quick bite. Food was strictly prohibited in the library, as was making out.

Brett sighed heavily and chewed on her crumbly granola bar. Normally on Sunday, the library was packed with frantic Waverly Owls cramming for Monday-morning tests or rushing to finish papers. But during Jan Plan, the library was nearly deserted, except for a table of freshman nerds in the corner, huddled over what looked like architectural blueprints for a space station.

The party had been a disaster. First, her fight with Sebastian, which she was trying really hard not to think about. Then, she'd gotten the e-mail from the dean citing her for being at the party. She blamed Sebastian for the fact that she'd been so distracted she'd left without her scarf. Another thing to be annoyed at him about. She'd had to slink into Stansfield Hall this morning, along with half a dozen other guilty-faced Owls, to claim it from the makeshift lost and found that the dean had—deviously—set up right outside his office door.

Chrissy was taking a trip to some giant fabric store outside Albany, but Brett had begged off at the last minute. She couldn't deal with Sebastian's exes anymore. Maybe they could do the rest of the project separately.

"You're Brett Messerschmidt, right?" Brett looked up from her giant book of boring mid-nineteenth-century French art to see a slender Asian girl in slim-fitting dark jeans tucked into a pair of high black boots. Her silky black hair hung down almost to her butt. She was vaguely familiar, but Brett couldn't think of her name.

"Yeeess?" Brett raised an eyebrow, not sure where this was going.

The girl stepped back and took Brett in from head to toe. Brett felt like she was at a casting call from the way the girl was evaluating everything from her flowered Juicy Couture waffle shirt to her baggy, ultra-comfortable J. Crew boyfriend jeans. Ironic, now that she wasn't sure she even had a boyfriend. Brett defensively touched her hand to her cheek to cover the tiny

pimple that had appeared yesterday. "You're junior class prefect, aren't you?"

"Yes," Brett replied, tapping her Salvatore Ferragamo
ankle boot impatiently against the table leg. She was prefect
for now—who knew what the new dean would have to say to
her tomorrow morning? "Is there something I can help you
with?"

The girl shrugged. Her skin was annoyingly perfect. "No,
you're just not what we expected."

"*We?*" Brett glanced around her, determined she must be
the subject of some stupid Jan Plan version of *Punk'd*.

"Oh, sorry. I'm Sylvia Ng. I used to go out with Sebastian."
Sylvia pulled a copy of *The New Yorker* from her Louis Vuitton
tote bag and returned it to the wall of periodicals, which, Brett
knew, weren't supposed to be circulated. "I was just talking to
Leila Rodriguez, and we realized that, even though we don't
really think you're Sebastian's type or anything, we think it's
cute that he's so, you know. Into you."

Brett shook her head, trying to clear her brain. "How do you
know that?"

Sylvia exaggeratedly rolled her eyes. "The other day he told,
like, every girl he'd ever hooked up with that he had a girlfriend now. At least, like, me and Leila, and Leigh, and . . ."

Brett felt like she had a nasty-tasting pill lodged in her
throat. The call log in Sebastian's phone. He'd been calling all
those girls—to tell them he was off the market? Why had he
done that? Her stomach dropped as she realized the answer.
Because of her. Because she'd flipped out on him after the Tricia

Rieken appearance. He'd gone out of his way to make sure it didn't happen again. For her sake.

And she'd been a complete bitch to him in return.

"Excuse me," Brett murmured, getting to her feet and grabbing her coat. She didn't even bother to return the art book to its shelf. Why had she been so quick to assume the worst? She had no reason not to trust him, and yet she hadn't even given him a chance to explain.

Brett raced out of the library, earning her a cranky warning from Mrs. Birdsall, and practically jogged over to Sebastian's dorm, slowing down only to catch her breath at the front door. The senior guys watching some lame Seth Rogen movie in the common room stared at her as she stalked by. When she got to his door, she paused. What was she going to say? She'd promised not to do this again. Was she determined to ruin every relationship she got into?

The door opened. Sebastian stood there, shirtless, in a pair of black Calvin Klein pajama bottoms. On his stereo, opera music was playing. "Were you ever going to knock? Or you planning on standing in the hall all day?"

Brett blinked, trying not to stare at Sebastian's lean, muscular chest. "I was trying to figure out the best way to apologize to you."

Sebastian stepped back, leaning against the back of his desk chair. "What'd you come up with?" His voice wasn't cold, exactly, but it was distant. Although she certainly deserved it.

"I'm sorry." Her heart was still beating like crazy from her run over here. She had to speak in short, clipped sentences. "I acted like an insane person. I'm really, really sorry I didn't give you a chance to explain. Or, rather, that I jumped to conclusions in the first place. It's just . . . I got a little . . . nervous, when I started to realize how many girls you've dated. I wasn't really sure how I fit in."

Sebastian pressed his lips together. "I told you how you fit in, remember? I told you that you were the only one who mattered."

"I know." Brett tried to take a deep breath of air. "I guess, the truth is . . ." She trailed off, not sure she wanted to admit this. But she had to be honest. She owed him that much. "I cheated on my last boyfriend. And he cheated on me. And so I'm not totally sure . . . I trust anyone anymore."

Sebastian shook his head. "Hey, crazy lady. I know you have a ton of baggage—I could tell that the first time I saw you."

Brett giggled. "You could not." She saw the framed photograph of his grandmother on his desk, standing in front of some tiny Italian restaurant. How could she ever have doubted him? Maybe because things were going so well between them, she panicked and took the easy way out—running before she got in too deep. But as he smiled at her with his full lips, she realized she was already in too deep.

And she liked it.

"Here's the thing," Sebastian said, touching Brett's elbow and pulling her toward him. "It's not that hard. You like me. I like you. Done."

Brett unwound the kelly green scarf she'd hastily thrown around her neck. "Do you really think it's that simple?"

"With you?" Sebastian shrugged his shoulders, suddenly looking a little embarrassed, like he had over Christmas break when she'd found the worn-out teddy bear on his bookshelf. "Yeah, I do. It's not like I've, you know, ever felt this way before."

An explosion of warmth spread through Brett's body. "Really?" she squeaked.

"Really." Sebastian's dark eyes met Brett's, and the warmth deepened. She stepped toward him, touching his arm with her gloved hand. He grinned at her, his familiar, amused smile. "Why else would I put up with your general craziness?"

Brett tucked her head against his strong chest. He smelled like he'd just stepped out of the shower. "Does that mean I'm forgiven?"

"Definitely not," Sebastian replied firmly, putting his hands on her shoulders and squeezing gently. "You've got to work a little harder than that." But then his fake frown turned back into his devilish grin.

Brett sighed happily and stepped toward him, until their bodies were almost, but not quite, touching. "I have a few ideas about how to make it up to you."

OwlNet   Instant Message Inbox

BennyCunningham: Did U see Jenny this morning? She still hasn't
                      heard from the dean.

SageFrancis: That's messed up. Getting caught is bad
                  enough. But when the party thrower gets off
                  free, that's ridiculous.

BennyCunningham: U know it's because the dean's son's in love
                      with her.

SageFrancis: Or her giant boobs.

BennyCunningham: Those are unfair, too!

A SMART OWL NEVER APPROACHES THE DEAN
WITHOUT A PLAN.

Jenny stared miserably at the untouched hummus wrap on her tray. She had absolutely no appetite. She'd come late to lunch, having spent the entire morning in the art studio. It was the perfect place to avoid just about everyone, and Jenny had the entire, loftlike space to herself. But she just couldn't concentrate on her artwork. She was completely consumed with anxiety, checking her phone every five minutes to see if the dean had e-mailed her. Nothing. As crazy as it was, she kept hoping that maybe he'd saved a special punishment, just for her, for planning the party. But it looked like Isaac had completely saved her.

Across the dining hall, Benny and Verena sat at a small, round table. As Jenny headed toward them, they both stood up and pointedly headed to the tray return, even though their sandwiches were only half eaten. Jenny sighed at the brush-off. At least Callie was too distracted with Easy's return to be annoyed with Jenny. When they were at the bathroom sinks that morning, Callie had started brushing her teeth without putting any toothpaste on her brush. Jenny had to wave her tube of Crest in front of her roommate's face before she realized it. Callie was normally slow in the mornings, but this was something else.

Across the dining hall, a table of freshmen whispered and pointed at Jenny. It made her stomach turn. She stood up, returned her tray with her uneaten lunch, and stormed out of the dining hall.

Five minutes later, she found herself knocking on the door of Dean Dresden's office.

"Come in," his voice bellowed. Timidly, she pushed open the door. His office was completely transformed from the other day. The walls had been painted a rich sunflower yellow—the color Jenny had suggested that first day she met with him. The shelves had been filled with books of all shapes and sizes, and an antique globe sat on a dark wood stand in the corner. An elegantly aged Oriental rug covered most of the previously bare hardwood floor.

"Oh, hello, Jenny." Dean Dresden looked up from the new flat-screen monitor that sat in the middle of his desk. He leaned back in his chair. "How are you doing today?"

Jenny blinked at the dean's friendliness. There was no trace of anger in his distinguished-looking face. "I'm . . . okay." She stepped forward, nervously adjusting her knee-length pleated skirt. "But I just wanted to ask you something."

"Ask away."

Jenny took a deep breath. Her boots were leaving wet footprints on his expensive-looking rug. "I was wondering when I was going to, um, get my punishment for the party."

The dean took a giant breath and clicked something with his mouse. "Jenny, let's not worry about this one." For the first time, she noticed a hard edge in his grayish-green eyes, as if he were the one who was slightly uncomfortable.

"But . . . why?"

The dean nodded slowly, smoothing down his navy-and-yellow-striped tie. The window behind him looked out over the quad, and Jenny could see a bunch of kids building a giant snow fort. She wished she were out there with them right now. But then she realized a few of them were probably on academic probation. And it was all her fault. "Look, I know you're a good kid, and I believe in second chances."

"But what about everyone else?" If Jenny deserved a second chance, so did all the other people who got busted. "What about their second chances?"

"Academic probation means they're getting a second chance." The dean pursed his lips. "Isaac said you didn't know anything about the party. Was that not true?"

Jenny's face flushed bright red. It was sweet of Isaac to cover for her, and it was definitely flattering that he wanted to protect her. But that didn't mean it was fair. For a moment, she thought about what fessing up would mean. It would mean having to tell her father she was on academic probation. It would mean she couldn't mess up again.

But if she kept her mouth shut, everyone would continue to resent her. Everyone, including all the friends she'd struggled to make here at Waverly.

She took a deep breath. "Dean Dresden, Isaac only said that

to protect me. The party was all my fault. If I hadn't suggested it to Isaac, it wouldn't have happened in the first place."

The dean stood up and leaned over his desk. He was staring at Jenny curiously. "Jenny, are you sure you know what you're saying?"

Jenny nodded her head firmly, even though she couldn't quite meet the dean's eyes. "Yes. The party was my idea, and I'm so sorry about it. I don't deserve any special treatment. I'd like to take the probation along with everyone else."

Guiltily, she wondered if Isaac was sweeping up broken glass and washing out wineglasses. They'd planned to send everyone home with enough time to clean up the party before the dean and his wife returned, but obviously that plan hadn't worked. "And if you need someone to help clean up your house, I'm happy to do it."

Dean Dresden shook his head sternly and rubbed his chin. "In all my years at various schools, I think this is a first. A student coming to me, asking to be punished." He shook his head, appraising Jenny, looking surprised but maybe—just maybe—a little impressed. "But, as you know, this party was a serious lapse in judgment. My daughter was almost gravely injured."

"I realize that," Jenny said softly, staring at her toes.

The dean cleared his throat. "I'll see you Monday morning at eight A.M., along with everybody else." His voice was stern.

Jenny smiled weakly, grateful it was all over. Being on probation wasn't going to be fun, but at least she could look people in the eye again.

It had never felt so good to be in trouble.

A WAVERLY OWL KNOWS THAT IT'S NOT ALWAYS

EASY TO ERASE THE PAST.

Tinsley woke up late on Sunday morning, the brilliant noon sun peeking through the broken window blind. Her mouth felt like some animal had died in it—a sensation that, as a vegetarian, was all the more offensive to her. She grabbed the almost-empty bottle of Evian next to her bed and took a swig, then quickly swallowed two Advils. Her head was pounding.

She rolled out of bed, her bare feet cold against the hardwood floor. The room was empty, and Brett's bed was neatly made. Tinsley raised the blinds, yawning. Last night, a fresh snow had fallen, and the quad was filled with happy Waverly Owls, playing some kind of capture-the-flag game. Although she normally didn't go for spirit-building campus activities, right now she kind of wished she could throw on her snow boots and tackle someone into the snow.

Preferably, a lying, two-faced, spoiled-brat dean's daughter.

The worst part wasn't that she was in trouble—she'd been in trouble plenty of times before. It was that she had been stupid enough to throw away what she had with Julian for someone like Isla. Someone who would stab her in the back the first chance she got. She still couldn't believe that after selling her out, Isla had the nerve to claim that Tinsley would have done the same thing to her.

The more Tinsley thought about it, though, the more she realized that once upon a time, maybe she would have. After she dropped Julian's lighter and started the fire that burned down the barn on Miller's farm that fall, she'd maneuvered to pin the whole thing on Jenny. Just because Julian had liked Jenny. It was stupid and childish, but Tinsley had learned her lesson.

And there was a reason she'd changed, for the better. Julian.

She flipped through the printouts she'd made of the photos, looking at the all the beautiful pictures of her and Isla. They were gorgeous, all right, but now they seemed so pointless. It was two pretty, attention-grabbing girls acting like prima donnas in front of the entire student population of Waverly. It had been an excuse to look beautiful and show off, and nothing more.

Tinsley paused at one photo. Her, alone, wearing the red bikini and placing a top hat on the snowman. She had her face tilted toward the camera, and she was laughing. It was a goofy picture, more cute than sexy—she was giggling hysterically, and, despite the bikini, she kind of looked like a kid who loved to play in the snow. But suddenly she knew there was only one person she wanted to see it. She tore the rest of the printouts in half, tossing the pieces into her trash can. She'd take her time deleting every single one of the pictures from her camera later.

Without bothering to shower, she jumped into her favorite pair of True Religion jeans. Then she crammed her feet into her tennis sneakers and pulled on her puffy red Guess jacket over her black Calvin Klein tank top. On her way out the door, she didn't even glance in the mirror.

Julian was just stepping out the front door of his dorm when Tinsley raced up. He had on a navy knit cap with a wide red stripe, pulled down low on his forehead. "Hey," Tinsley said nervously, slowing down. A black leather camera bag was slung over his shoulder. "Where are you going?"

Julian didn't pause as he descended the brick steps leading down from his dorm. He gave Tinsley a noncommittal smile. "Meeting up with Alan. Working on our movie."

"Listen, can we talk?" Tinsley stepped in front of him so he was forced to stop.

"Funny you want to talk now." He paused, staring straight into Tinsley's eyes. His golden-brown eyes gazed at her as if she were a stranger, and Tinsley's heart sunk. "You weren't too interested in it the other night when I wanted to talk."

"Please don't be like that. I'm sorry." Tinsley's ankles were freezing, and she suddenly felt stupid, standing in front of the freshmen boys' dorm without any socks on, begging forgiveness from the guy she'd so stupidly dumped.

"Sorry for what? For breaking up with me because I hated the idea of having the entire male population of the school, which has, by the way, been in love with you for practically forever, gawk at pictures of your nearly naked body?" He crossed his arms over his chest and stared into the distance. Tinsley could see the snowman in front of the gym that she and Isla had used in their first photo shoot. Someone had stolen the sticks that had been his arms, and he looked sad without them. "Because someone newer and more interesting came along?"

"That's not what happened," Tinsley insisted, feeling her stomach start to quake. "I just . . . didn't want to be one of those, you know. Sweatpants couples."

"Sweatpants couples?" Julian's eyes widened. He pulled a pair of sunglasses from his pocket, and Tinsley reached out to touch his sleeve. She couldn't let him put sunglasses on—she needed to see his familiar brown eyes, she needed to tell what he was thinking. He left them in his pocket but stepped away from Tinsley, letting her hand fall back to her side. "What does that even mean?"

"You know." Tinsley shuffled her feet. Her tennis shoes were slippery against the snow. "Those couples who spend all their time together watching movies and eating Cheez Doodles and missing out on everything."

"You're right," Julian replied sarcastically. "That sounds exactly like us."

Tinsley shook her head. It did sound silly now, and she wished she could turn back the clock and tell him about everything earlier, before things got so messed up. "And they get fat, because they just order in pizza all the time. And then they can only wear sweatpants, because they're fat and lazy."

Julian turned to face Tinsley. He looked shocked. "Is that what you think I want? To steal you from all your friends and make you fat and lazy?"

"No!"

Julian started walking away from the dorm, and Tinsley was forced to follow him. They passed a couple of underclassmen carrying black musical instrument cases. "You're twisting my words when I'm trying to apologize."

"I'm trying to understand you, Tinsley." He shook his head slowly as he stared straight ahead. Tinsley had to hurry to keep up with his long strides. "Because, you know, you can never just tell me what you're feeling. Why didn't you say this to me *before* you broke up with me?" He pulled his knit cap lower down on his head. "Three weeks ago, you were breaking up with me because I wasn't a virgin—and you didn't give me a reason then, either. Or a chance to explain."

"I . . ." Tinsley opened her mouth, but nothing else came out. He was right, in a way. But that was only part of the story. Two overfed squirrels scampered across the path and Tinsley fought the urge to kick snow at them.

Julian stopped walking. He took a deep breath as he played with the zipper on his coat. The dimple beneath his lips was nowhere in sight. "Look. I really like you. I might even be in love with you. But I can't keep doing this. You get mad at me. You don't tell me why. You break up with me. You come back and apologize. Then it starts all over again."

"You're breaking up . . . with me?" Tinsley's knees buckled. Further up the path, she saw the bench where she'd first met Isla. She wished it was closer, because she felt like she might pass out. It couldn't be over with Julian. Not for real.

"You broke up with me, remember?" Julian took a deep breath. "I'm just not giving you a chance to do it again." He turned to walk away.

"Wait!" Tinsley felt her heart in her mouth. He couldn't leave her like this.

"I'm sorry," Julian said, his voice sadder than she'd ever heard. He leaned forward, and Tinsley's heart leaped. But he just pressed his lips to her cheek and gave her a quick peck before he spun around and walked, very quickly, away.

Tinsley watched him walk down the path until he disappeared into a cluster of people at the steps of Maxwell. The photo of herself in her red bikini was still in her pocket, but she was too shocked, and too proud, to race after him now. Instead, she headed back to his dorm and slipped it under his door.

Even if he didn't want it, it was his, and his alone.

IsaacDresden: My dad said you came to see him today. Why'd you do that?

JennyHumphrey: I had to. It was really nice of you to protect me, but the party was my idea. I should get in trouble along with everyone else.

IsaacDresden: I still think you're crazy, but oddly enough, I think you scored points with Dad for it.

JennyHumphrey: What about points with you?

IsaacDresden: You're already way ahead in my book.

JennyHumphrey: What about U? R U in trouble?

IsaacDresden: Grounded. Indefinitely.

JennyHumphrey: Can you sneak out for coffee? I feel like I still owe you one.

IsaacDresden: Good. I'd like to keep seeing you—indefinitely.

BennyCunningham: I was just in the dean's office and you won't guess what I heard.

SageFrancis: What were U doing there?

BennyCunningham: Picking up my coat. And dropping off brownies. Whatever. Do U want 2 know what I heard or not?

SageFrancis: What, that the dean's no Marymount? That he's letting Easy Walsh back into Waverly cuz he saved his little girl's life?

BennyCunningham: Bitch. So U already know?

SageFrancis: Everyone does. Wonder what that means for Callie.

BennyCunningham: I'll tell you one thing it means—she's gonna have some competition for EZ. I think Isla may have a crush on her knight in shining armor.

SageFrancis: Told you Jan Plan wouldn't be boring.

Blair Waldorf, Serena van der Woodsen,

Nate Archibald, Dan Humphrey, and

Vanessa Abrams went off to live their lives.

Now, they're coming home for the holidays.

A lot can change in a few months . . .

but some things never do.

Turn the page for a sneak peek of

I will always love you

a new gossip girl hardcover
featuring the original cast

gossipgirl.net

Disclaimer: All the real names of places, people, and events have been altered or abbreviated to protect the innocent. Namely, me.

| topics | sightings | your e-mail | post a question |

Hey people!

The more things change, the more they stay the same.

For years, New York City—the center of the universe, the place where anything can happen—was our home. But we've moved beyond our uniform-required, single-sex schools and into bastions of higher education around the country. Yes, it finally happened: We went to college. For the past few months, we've been surrounded by people who don't know who we've hooked up with, who don't remember the time we wet our pants on the playground in kindergarten. We've learned new things and made new friends and maybe even met the loves our lives. We've changed.

Or at least, *some* of us have. Others are just as fabulous as always. Take **B,** heading to Vermont to spend a perfect holiday with her perfect Yale boyfriend and his perfect family. That girl always had her eye on the prize. . . . And speaking of prizes, what's rumored SAG nominee **S** doing these days? Formerly worshipped by her Constance Billard class-mates, she's now followed by paparazzi and a posse of fellow movie starlets. No matter where she is or what she does, **S** will *always* be the center of attention.

Then there are the people who've tried their hardest to change: **N** is on a sailing trip around the world. But as we all know from reading Kant in our freshman seminars, no man is an island. He'll be back. Then there's **D,** scratching out poetry in his Moleskine notebook in the Pacific Northwest. It may look like a total lifestyle change, but he still insists on Folgers instead of French press in the coffee capital of the U.S. He also spends every waking moment attempting to Skype his shaven-headed, ultra independent filmmaker girlfriend, **V,** who's at NYU and seems to almost . . . have *hair*. And friends. Lastly there's **C,** last seen with a pack of flannel-wearing, very rugged boys. Is he into a new type, or has he gone through yet another reinvention? That man puts Madonna to shame.

Everyone's back in town for the holidays, and this winter break is guaranteed to be filled with makeups, breakups, and shakeups. Lucky for you, I'm going to report *everything* worth reporting. Let the reunion begin.

sightings:

B on a train from New Haven to Montpelier, VT, looking very out of place in a sea of flannel . . . **S** with three identical girls, on the red carpet for a premiere. . . . **V** and some friends from NYU, including her very young, very cute teaching assistant, at a film-screening party in Bushwick. Is someone trying to get extra credit? . . . **D** and his little sister, **J,** splitting a plate of chocolate-chip pancakes at one of those curiously packed diners on upper Broadway. . . . **C** and a group of cowboy boot–clad guys ordering sodas at the lounge at the **Tribeca Star**. Ride 'em cowboy!

Break the rules

Remember, you don't technically live under your parents' roof anymore. You've already indulged them in holiday merry-making: Scrabble with the siblings, kissing Grandma, and decorating cookies that nobody's going to eat. Which means now is the time to use all your pent-up energy to party. Remember, you can always reform after January 1—that's what resolutions are for. So go out, have fun, and most of all, show your former besties and former flames just how much *better* you've become.

Besides, now that you know I'm watching, aren't you just dying to put on a show? Thought so.

You know you love me,

All B wants for Christmas

"You awake, Scout?"

Blair Waldorf awoke from a nap to the sight of her boyfriend, Pete Carlson, gazing down at her. Pete smiled his adorable, lop-sided smile. His eyes were a yellowish brown and reminded Blair of her cat, Kitty Minky's.

She threw the Black Watch plaid duvet to the foot of the couch and discreetly checked for drool with her index finger. She *loved* being woken up by Pete, especially when he called her by an adorable nickname. Currently, it was Scout because she'd directed him and his three older brothers to the best Douglas fir Christmas tree, deep in the woods of the Carlson's expansive Woodstock, Vermont estate.

"Of course I am," Blair lied, sitting up and yawning. Why sleep when her waking life was so much *better*?

"Good." Pete settled next to her on the couch, tenderly push-ing Blair's long bangs off her small, foxlike face. Her hair was a little shaggier than she'd like, but she simply didn't trust any of the hair salons in New Haven. Besides, what were unkempt bangs when she was with a guy who loved her?

"Have any dreams? You were making these little growls in your sleep. It was cute." Pete pulled the blanket off the floor and draped it over their legs.

"Oh." Blair frowned. She was *growling*?

In truth, she'd been having a lot of weird dreams lately. Last night, she'd woken up and thought she was at a sleepover at her old best friend Serena van der Woodsen's house, only to find herself all alone in the guest bedroom of the Carlson's.

Maybe it was just homesickness. After all, she hadn't seen Serena since August, she didn't have a home in New York anymore, and no one in her family was even in the U.S. this week. Her father, Harold, was celebrating Christmas in France with his boyfriend and their adopted twins. Her stepbrother, Aaron, was spending the break on a kibbutz in Israel. Her mother; stepfather; brother, Tyler; and baby sister, Yale, had moved to LA back in August, to a gigantic, tacky Pacific Palisades mansion that they were making even bigger and more tacky. While the renovations were taking place, they were spending the holidays in the South Pacific, visiting the islands that Eleanor Rose, in a fit of pregnancy-induced mania last spring, had bought for each member of the family. Blair had been somewhat tempted to tag along, if only to see her baby sister, the least fucked-up member of her tragically absurd family.

Not to mention pay a visit to Blair Island.

But once she'd been invited to spend Christmas with the Carlsons, she felt it was her duty as a girlfriend to go.

"I was just dreaming about you. Us. I'm just so happy." Blair sighed contentedly as she gazed into the orange fire roaring in the wood burning stove across the room. Outside, a thin blanket of snow covered the ground.

"Me too." Pete ruffled her hair and pulled her face into his for a kiss.

"You taste nice," Blair breathed, letting her body relax into Pete's muscular arms.

It was funny how things worked out. When she arrived at Yale, Blair discovered that her roommate, Alana Hoffman, sang a cappella all the time. Blair would wake up to Alana singing "Son of a Preacher Man" to her collection of teddy bears. Avoiding her room, Blair spent a lot of time in the library, where Pete was writing a paper for his Magical Realism in the Caribbean class. They'd exchanged flirty glances, and finally Pete invited her for coffee.

It was amazing how *easy* everything could be with Pete. For the first time in Blair's nineteen years, her life felt like it made sense. She loved her classes, lived in a house of boys who adored her, had an adoring, handsome boyfriend, and had even found a surrogate family in the Carlsons.

For the past few days, they'd spent every waking hour with the family: His former U.S. Senator dad, Chappy; his Boston debutante mom, Jane; his three older brothers, their wives, and assorted nephews and nieces Blair couldn't even try to keep straight. It sounded like a nightmare, but it was great. His dad was barrel-chested and red-faced and told bad jokes in a way that made everyone crack up, and his mom would randomly recite poetry at the dinner table without being drunk. The brothers were friendly and smart, their wives were nice, and even the kids were polite. So far, it had been a perfect holiday.

And it was about to get even better. To celebrate the New Year, Chappy had booked the entire family at an exclusive resort in Costa Rica. Obviously, Blair could do without the rainforest adventure part, but she'd heard the beaches were pristine, the sun was hot and the villas had the most incredible mattresses.

Just then, there was a knock at the door. "You kids decent?" Pete's brother Jason called as he entered. He had the same lanky frame as Pete. Tall, blond, and handsome, all four of the Carlson brothers—Everett, Randy, Jason, and Pete—looked like they could be quadruplets, even though there was a two year age difference between them. A second year law student at UPenn, Jason was the second youngest of the Carlson brothers. He was adorable, and Blair would've had a crush on him if she wasn't dating Pete.

At least she has a backup.

"We're playing charades. Your presence has been requested."

"Do we have to?" Blair suppressed a groan. It was cute in theory, but they'd played Charades, Pictionary, or Scrabble the last three nights.

Maybe they should shake it up with some Truth or Dare.

"And guess who's requested you on his team again?" Jason smirked, flashing Blair the trademark white-toothed Carlson smile. "Our dad loves you!"

"Aw, that's cute!" Blair said, mustering her enthusiasm. They'd be at the resort soon, so she might as well continue being as polite and friendly as possible to his family. She followed Pete through the wide arching hallway that led to the kitchen. A large wood stove hunkered in the corner opposite two massive Sub-Zero refrigerators. Several overstuffed yellow chairs sat in front of a large dormer window, each one containing a different member of the family. Pete's father Chappy stood in front of the group.

"Scout!" he called happily as he spotted Blair and Pete.

"Hi, Mr. Carlson." Blair smiled warmly.

"I already claimed you, so back off, boys," Chappy said jovially to Pete's brothers, who all smiled politely back at her. "I'm telling you, Scout, I don't know how I'm going to manage without you next week," Chappy continued.

"Oh, well, I'm sure we can play on the beach or something," Blair said. She blushed. "Play charades on the beach," she clarified.

"Yeah, but what'll I do without my favorite teammate?" Chappy shook his head sorrowfully. "No offense, Jane." He cupped his hand over Blair's ear. "My wife cheats," he whispered, winking at his wife. Jane Carlson had wheat-blond hair cut in a sensible bob and was tall, with an athletic frame. Only the deep wrinkles in her forehead made her seem old enough to be Pete's mom, and they didn't make her look ancient so much as friendly.

"I do cheat, I'll be the first to admit it," Jane said merrily. "I'm glad you're on the straight and narrow." She winked at Blair.

But Blair was still stuck on the part of Chappy's sentence that implied she *wouldn't* be in Costa Rica with them. She'd bought five new Eres bikinis for the occasion. They made the most of the five pounds she'd gained from Yale's meal plan. "*Without me?*" Blair repeated stupidly.

"I mean, I'd bring you along, but we've got a saying in the Carlson family . . ." Chappy began, his eyes shining, as if he were about to deliver a stump speech. "I believe, when it comes to vacations, in the *no ring, no bring* rule."

"It's the Carlson curse." Jason sighed, elbowing Blair in the ribs sympathetically. Blair stepped away. While it was true she'd never *officially* been invited to Costa Rica, she'd been invited for Christmas, for God's sake. Wasn't that even more exclusive than a beach holiday? And why *not* invite her? After all, she'd brought Nate Archibald, her high school boyfriend, on her family vacations for years and it wasn't like she'd been married to him.

Except in her dreams.

"Blair, we love you and we want you in our family for years to come, but I need to be a stickler on this," Chappy explained sympathetically, as if she were one of his constituents, arguing over some impossible and arcane rule. "I've raised four boys, and while they've behaved around you, honestly, these gentlemen cause more theatrics when it comes to ladies than the Yale School of Drama," he finished.

"Maybe you could get together with your girlfriends and have a girl's adventure!" Pete's sister-in-law Sarah piped up from the corner of the room, stroking her eight-months-pregnant belly. "I remember when I heard the Carlson rule, I had a great time with the Theta girls. We went to Cancun!" A look of happy reminiscence crossed Sarah's heart-shaped face.

"You did?" Randy asked, shooting a look at Sarah. "I didn't know that."

"All I'm saying is that Blair should have her own fun." Sarah winked conspiratorially at Blair.

"More hot chocolate, anyone?" Pete's mother asked, excusing herself.

"Sorry, son!" Chappy said, genuinely sounding remorseful as he clapped Pete on the back. "Sorry, Scout!"

Blair narrowed her eyes at a painting that hung over the fireplace, of a ship in what looked like an exceptionally violent storm. What type of fucking art was that to hang in a house? And what the fuck was up with that stupid nickname? Scout?

Out would have been more appropriate.

"Blair, I'm sorry," Pete said simply. "I thought you understood . . ."

"What? I knew I wasn't coming," Blair lied, smiling fakely. Her stomach was churning wildly. For a brief second, she wanted to excuse herself, run to the second floor bathroom, and puke everything she'd eaten for the past five days. But she didn't.

"Blair, darling, here's your hot chocolate. I made sure to put some extra marshmallows in there." Jane pushed the steaming mug into Blair's hands. "Won't you sit down?" She gestured to one of the comfortable overstuffed chairs.

"Thanks," Blair said. She squared her shoulders and turned to the waiting Carlson clan. "You all ready to play?" She forced herself to smile, a plan already forming.

"Maybe I *will* have a wild girls' weekend," she whispered to Pete. "I haven't been to New York all year." His face fell as he no doubt pictured all the fun she'd be having without him. Blair raised an eyebrow challengingly. After all, she was a woman. A Yale woman. She had places to go.

And games to play.

make new friends, but keep the old . . .

"This came from the man at the other end of the bar," the skinny bartender slash model said as he proffered a glass of champagne.

"Thanks." Serena van der Woodsen glanced down the long, dark oak bar of Saucebox, the new lounge in the just-opened hotel on Thompson Street. Breckin O'Dell, an actor she vaguely remembered meeting a few times, held up his own glass of champagne and saluted her. Serena nodded, brought the glass to her lips and took a sip, even though she preferred vodka.

"Oh my God, you should totally date him. His agent has ridiculous connections," Amanda Atkins said, pulling on the sleeve of Serena's black The Row scoopneck jersey dress in excitement. "Can we get some shots down here?" she called to the bartender. Serena smiled indulgently. Amanda was an eighteen-year-old recent LA transplant best known for her role in a dorky sitcom about a girl from Paris who moves to a farm in Tennessee to live with her redneck uncle. Recently, though, she'd been cast in an indie film and was trying to break free from her good-girl reputation.

Another shot and she's almost there.

"Maybe," Serena said unconvincingly. She stared at the bubbles fizzing to the top of her glass as if they held the secrets to the universe. If she looked around her, she'd see tons of Breckin O'Dell look-alikes, no doubt wishing *they'd* been the ones to buy Serena van der Woodsen—*the* Serena van der Woodsen—a drink. Instead, they buzzed around Amanda, and her other two actress-friends, Alysia and Alison. They called themselves the three A's, even though Alysia's name was actually Jennifer.

The three A's were admittedly a little shallow, but they were also goofy and fun and never turned down a party. Usually Serena had a blast hanging out with them, but tonight, she felt a little . . . off. Her parents had just left for St. Barths, while her brother, Eric, was spending the winter break in Australia with a girl who'd been a visiting student at Brown last year. It wasn't like she wanted to spend New Year's Eve with her family, but she also didn't like waking up in their huge Fifth Avenue apartment alone. Serena downed her champagne in one gulp, telling herself that she just needed to have fun.

And, after all, she is the expert.

"Hey, you're that farm chick!" One guy stuttered, not looking Amanda in the eye. His hair was gelled and he was wearing a pink and white striped button-down. It was clear that he'd had to bribe the bouncer to get into the bar.

"Yes," Amanda sighed. "But, actually, I have to stand over here now." Amanda took two steps away, as Alysia and Alison snorted in laughter. Serena offered the guy a sympathetic smile. Even though she was beautiful, Serena was never mean.

An infuriating combination.

"God, you'd think Knowledge would know to not to let guys like that in. Did you see his hair? It was like, sprayed on." Amanda flipped her extensions over her shoulder as she named the beefy bouncer whose job was to keep Saucebox as exclusive as possible, even though, to Serena, it felt exactly the same as every other bar she'd been to recently.

"Serena?"

Serena whirled around, ready to have another one of those *so great to see you* conversations with someone she'd probably met once. Instead, she saw a familiar, smiling face that immediately took her back in time.

"Oh my God, Iz!" Serena squealed excitedly. She slid off the smooth bar stool and threw her arms around Isabel Coates, a fellow Constance Billard alum who'd gone to Rollins College down in Florida. She was super tan and had highlights in her shoulder-length blond hair. She automatically looked over Isabel's shoulder, sure she'd see Kati Farkas, Isabel's best friend and constant side-kick. Isabel and Kati had done everything together back in high school. Kati even turned down admission to Princeton so they wouldn't have to be separated. But instead of Kati, a girl with a ski-jump nose and straight brown hair stood next to Isabel.

"This is my girlfriend, Casey," Isabel announced proudly.

"Oh." Wait, did that mean *girlfriend* girlfriend? Serena noticed Isabel's hand intertwined with Casey's.

"We met in a woman's studies class." Isabel smiled adoringly at Casey.

There's her answer.

"This is Serena van der Woodsen. We went to school together," she explained.

"Nice to meet you, Casey," Serena said, holding out her hand to the tall girl, who took it gingerly.

"Nice to meet you, too. I haven't seen any of your movies," Casey announced self-importantly.

"How's Kati?" Serena asked.

Isabel sighed and shook her head. "She has this like, football player boyfriend and is pledging a sorority that wears pink sweatsuits to class. It's awful," she sighed disdainfully. "Casey and I pretty much do our own thing. But what about *you*? I saw your movie. You were pretty good," Isabel allowed.

"Thanks," Serena said, resisting the urge to roll her eyes. "Things are okay. Just working a lot. We're filming a sequel to *Breakfast at Fred's* that's coming out in summer, so that's fun . . ." Serena trailed off. Even though she'd been on the cover of the October issue of *Vanity Fair*, part of her felt stuck. After all, she'd come home from her big premiere to her same pink childhood bedroom in her parents' sprawling penthouse. If possible, she almost felt *less* grown up than she had last year, especially since she now had an agent and a publicist who told her exactly what to wear, what to say, and who to be seen with.

"Sounds great!" Isabel cooed. "Anyway, I was just showing Casey all the old places we used to go. Remember how we used to like, spend hours trying things on at Barney's? I just can't believe we were ever so *young*. Things have changed a lot," she mused, nuzzling her blond-highlighted head against Casey.

"Things *have* changed," Serena agreed. Less than a year ago, she and Blair and Kati and Isabel would meet before school to smoke Merits on the Met steps and imagine their lives in college. Now Blair was a poli-sci major at Yale, Isabel was a lesbian, Kati was a sorority girl, and Serena was a movie star.

"So, have you seen anyone?" Isabel asked.

"No." Serena shook her head. For her, only two people really mattered: Blair and Nate. She and Blair had tried to keep in touch, and once Serena had sent Blair a package full of Wolford stockings, black and white cookies, in a Barney's bag—all of Blair's favorite New York things. Blair had reciprocated with a stuffed bulldog wearing a Yale T-shirt. They'd send occasional e-mails and texts, but never anything long or involved. It was fine, though. Blair and Serena were the type of friends who could go weeks without speaking, then pick up right where they left off.

As for Nate . . . they hadn't talked since he left, to sail the world for a year. Serena wondered if she'd ever see him again. But she didn't want to think about that right now.

Or ever.

"Are you going to Chuck's New Year's party tomorrow night?" Isabel asked, draining the rest of her drink. "I mean, I know he's like, such a misogynist, but I figured, you can only protest so much, you know? I prepared Casey."

"Wait, didn't Chuck go to military school?" She hadn't

thought about Chuck—with his sketchy history, his trademark monogrammed scarf, or his questionable sexuality—for months. But the last she'd heard, after getting rejected from all twelve schools he'd applied to, he'd gone to some underground, in the middle of nowhere, academy. Of course her parents saw Chuck's parents socially, but they never mentioned him. It was an unspoken rule on the Upper East Side that parents didn't discuss their unsuccessful children.

"Who knows?" Isabel shrugged. "The party's on, though. I saw Laura Salmon at City Bakery this morning and she told me she spoke to Rain Hofstetter at some lame Constance alum tea party that Mrs. M. organized. Thank god I missed that. But, anyway, I guess she talked to Chuck. I don't know. It's at the Tribeca Star. But I guess since you're a movie star and all, you probably have to host some MTV special or something, right?"

"Well . . ." Serena trailed off. In truth, she already had an invite to a party at Thaddeus Russell's Chelsea loft. Thaddeus had been her *Breakfast at Fred's* costar and was a true friend. But he wouldn't mind if she stopped by to say hi and then went off to Chuck's party.

"I'll be there," Serena chirped. She suddenly couldn't wait for New Year's Eve. How could she *not* go see her old high school crowd? While she may not have been thinking of them all that much recently, it wasn't like she'd forgotten them.

And they certainly haven't forgotten her.

gossip girl

I will always love you

The secret is out 11.3.09

Welcome to Poppy.

A poppy is a beautiful blooming red flower
(like the one on the spine of this book). It is also
the name of the home of your favorite books.

Poppy takes the real world and makes it
a little funnier, a little more fabulous.

Poppy novels are wild, witty, and inspiring.
They were written just for you.

So sit back, get comfy, and pick a Poppy.

poppy

www.pickapoppy.com